THE FEUD

THE FEUD

GILES A. LUTZ

DOUBLEDAY & COMPANY, INC.
GARDEN CITY, NEW YORK
1982

All of the characters in this book
are fictitious, and any resemblance
to actual persons, living or dead,
is purely coincidental.

Library of Congress Cataloging in Publication Data

Lutz, Giles A.
The feud.

I. Title.
PS3562.U83F4   813'.54
AACR2
ISBN: 0-385-17685-6
Library of Congress Catalog Card Number 81-43293
Copyright © 1982 by Giles A. Lutz
All Rights Reserved
Printed in the United States of America
First Edition

THE FEUD

CHAPTER 1

Jacob Keeley stood at the bank's window, watching Landers' traffic. It wasn't much this morning. The weather saw to that. A howling wind rode down the street, and people were hunched over as they braved it. They made their trips as brief as possible.

Keeley's shoulders were sagging, and his face was unhappy. It might have been the aftermath of a long, hard winter, and it could be just a general discontent with the town and the life it afforded. His father had been affluent enough to send him to San Francisco for schooling. It had been an idyllic life, then his father had suffered the heart attack. The attack had called Jacob back from school; worse, it had broken into his rapidly growing romance with Cynthia Dawson. He mentally groaned as he recalled his promises to Cynthia. "I won't be gone long, Cynthia. I'll be back before you know it."

It hadn't worked out that way. His father had lingered six months before he succumbed. Then there was that deathbed promise that Jacob would stay and run the bank his father had established.

Jacob stirred restlessly. Just thinking about that promise aroused his resentment against his father. Cynthia wouldn't wait much longer. Jacob could tell by the tone of her letters. Two years was a long time. The vision of a better life was rapidly slipping away from him. Cynthia came from a wealthy family. Jacob's background of a banking family had established him firmly with Cynthia's family. He hadn't been quite truthful. He had embellished that background, making it stronger than it was. Cyrus' bank wasn't much. Oh, it afforded a living, but it couldn't compare with the wealth of Cynthia's family.

Jacob groaned again at the thought of what would happen if her family ever found out that he had been lying. His tenuous hold on Cynthia would be snapped, and he couldn't stand the thought of that. The thoughts of those glorious days in San Francisco filtered through his head. They were forever gone, if he couldn't come up with a sum that would let him live in the manner he had let Cynthia's family believe. He had thought of selling the bank, but that sum would be insufficient to keep up his farce much longer. Those people in San Francisco knew how to live.

He shifted restlessly as he contrasted living in San Francisco with the drab life in Landers. He was trapped hopelessly unless he could see a way to return to San Francisco with sufficient money to re-establish the life he had known with Cynthia. He wanted to rail at the chains life threw about a man, holding him where he didn't want to be. He pounded a fist into a palm in sudden frustration. He might have been better off if he hadn't inherited this bank. He wasn't cut out to be a small-town banker.

He had argued with Cyrus, knowing from the onslaught he would lose. A dying man had all the strength against anything Jacob could raise. Life in Landers had been enough for Cyrus; it would be enough for Jacob. He didn't want to wind up as he remembered his father. Some mornings when he looked into a mirror, he could swear he was growing more and more to look like his father. His shoulders were becoming more bent, and that pinched look was beginning to steal into his face. He could rave at his reflection, and that didn't change a thing. Oh, if he could only throw it all up and leave for San Francisco. The more he explored that possibility, the more he saw how impossible it was. Oh, he could sell the bank, but the sum he would receive wasn't enough to live on for long. After that sum was gone, 'what was he going to do? He had no training for anything else. That stark realization frightened him. Jacob Keeley wasn't a man of great moral courage, and he couldn't face that bleak prospect. No, he was trapped in this hopeless, god-forsaken town. The bank would give him a comfortable living but nothing elaborate. His soul screamed in agony. He would spend the rest of his life threshing about in this trap.

He continued staring out of the window, not really seeing anything. Think, damn you, he berated himself. Daily, he had gone through that berating ever since his father's funeral two years ago. Nothing had occurred to him. He was in the heart of the money-making business, and he was utterly devoid of ideas.

The sound of a voice being cleared jerked his head about. Benson, the teller, stood importunately behind him. Charley Benson was a painfully thin man, his hair white, his face harassed. He had worked in this bank for better than twenty years, and the sight of him unleashed Keeley's feeling of rage. He'd be goddamned if he would end up like this. Benson and his father had gotten along well, but there was no such kindred feeling between him and Benson. Keeley detested the man, and Benson didn't have much better feeling for him. In fact, Keeley thought Benson was in fear of him. He should be, Keeley thought. He knows his job depends upon me.

"What is it, Benson?" he asked impatiently.

"It's the Hillory account, Mr. Keeley," Benson said apologetically.

"What about it?" Keeley snapped.

"Ben Hillory is overdue on his payment on his loan. He should have been in last week."

Keeley's forehead knit in an effort to recall the matter of which Benson spoke. "Did I handle it?" he asked impatiently.

"You did, sir. You accept or reject all loans. Hillory put up his forty acres as collateral."

Keeley's forehead smoothed. He remembered it now. The forty acres identified Hillory for him. Hillory was a big, bumbling man with a permanent defeated look on his countenance.

"Ah, yes," Keeley said. "You know the bank's policy. If Hillory is overdue, foreclose on him."

That seemed to cause Benson distress. "I thought you might consider giving him a little more time. Hillory tries so hard. Last winter hit him hard. He lost five of the ten herd of his cows."

Keeley made an impatient gesture. "Everybody went through the same winter. How long do you think the bank would last if it nursed all the weaklings?"

Benson's face went blank. "Then you want me to start foreclosure proceedings?"

"You catch on quick," Keeley said sarcastically. "You'll never get in trouble as long as you follow the bank's policy."

Benson cringed as he backed away. "Whatever you say, sir."

Keeley watched him retreat into his cage. Helpless old fool, he raged inwardly. He turned back to stare out of the window again. His fuming slowly ebbed. Where would this bank be if Benson gave heed to his soft feelings? So Hillory had gone through a tough winter. He wasn't alone. One such winter as the last was enough, but there had been two like winters in a row. Those winters had been punishing. Long periods of brutal cold and deep, frequent snowfalls. Cold and moisture were twin knockout blows. They hurt people and animals. Keeley had heard that the livestock loss was tremendous. The full extent of the loss wouldn't probably be known until the true arrival of spring. That kind of struggle took everything out of men and beasts, leaving little more than just enough strength for the difficult chore of survival. The surviving stock would be weak and feeble, and many of them wouldn't have enough strength left to rebuild enough energy to get into the summer. It was the same with people. The aged would be weak and listless, and the will to exist would noticeably wane.

Weather was always a cruel mocker. The calendar said it should be spring, but from the looks of this day, it seemed that winter was drawing a fresh breath for a new onslaught.

This kind of thinking was doing him no good. He'd better put his thoughts on something more soothing. He transferred his thoughts to Hillory's little dab of land. The bank would foreclose. That was as certain as tomorrow. Keeley wasn't sure what he would do with the land. Probably put it up for the highest bid. It was nothing to get worked up over. That small parcel of land wouldn't bring enough money to get in a sweat over.

The trend of his thoughts excited Keeley. If Cyrus had been an astute businessman, he would have spent his lifetime amassing land, big chunks of land. That's where the real money was. Why, if his father had started that policy when he first came to Wyoming, he would own enough property to buy the state.

Keeley felt his fingernails bite into his palms. It was too late to be thinking of that now. Cyrus had had that opportunity. It was all gone now.

He idly watched Grat Hagen come out of the saloon across the street. Hagen was a big burly man, and he was as tough as his appearance. Both Grat and his father were known for their ability to punish a bottle. That quality didn't help that infamous temper. Hagen paused to set his hat more firmly on his head against the onslaught of the wind.

Hagen started out again, and Keeley thought his step was unsteady. At his distance, he couldn't be certain. The wind tugging at Hagen could have its effect.

Hagen came to the corner and turned right around Arnold's store. His head was down, and he didn't see the man approaching him.

Keeley sucked in a breath. He didn't see how the threatening collision could be avoided. Both men's heads were down, and they walked briskly to escape the insidious cold.

Keeley watched with renewed interest. The second man was Jessie Kilmer. There was enough bad blood between the two men without an accidental collision stirring up the old animosity.

Kilmer plowed into Hagen, and even though Keeley couldn't hear the impact, he could see the results. Both were big men, and momentum was behind the impact.

Both men staggered. Hagen lost his footing on a decaying patch of snow, and he went down hard. He threw up both arms, trying to maintain his balance, and the wild upswing dislodged his hat. The wind caught it, sending it skittering down the street.

Now there was going to be one hell of a fight. If there was no actual insult intended, Hagen would build up the impact into one. There was an old and lasting feud between the two. It was well-based in legendary and actual violence. Hagen came from a cattle family, and that family detested everything the Kilmers stood for. The Kilmers were one of the biggest sheep raisers in Wyoming. They returned every shred of hatred the Hagens sent their way. Ten years ago the war had been an open fray. Men and animals had been slaughtered. The law fought valiantly to stem it, and Quint Raines, Landers' sheriff, had done yeoman's work in quelling the war. He had hired some men who could shoot and weren't afraid to. Those deputies had killed some men and sent others to jail. It seemed it took a certain amount of bloodshed, diluted by women's tears, to force some sense into men's heads.

Raines had manhandled peace into existence. It hadn't been an easy thing, and the old hatred hadn't died. But Raines had clubbed the contestants into submission. Oh, there had been numerous fistfights over the uneasy years, but no one had tried to use a gun again.

Keeley's eyes glittered as he watched Hagen climb unsteadily to his feet. He shouted something at Kilmer that Keeley couldn't hear, but the wrathful set of Hagen's face proclaimed how incensed he was.

Would the war start all over here? Keeley didn't know. At the time of the actual war, both Hagen and Kilmer were only kids, but youth was no guarantee that it wouldn't be poisoned by hatred.

Kilmer set himself for Hagen's rush. It might be a hell of a brawl until Raines got word and broke it up.

CHAPTER 2

Jessie Kilmer winced as the wind caught him. The damned stuff had the fangs of a killer wolf, ripping away at any exposed skin on a man's body. Even the sheepskin coat wasn't sufficient protection. Jessie turned up the collar and ducked his chin deep into it. The damned winter would never end. It was well into springtime, but seeing nothing but barren ground didn't bear it out. It was almost to the spring lambing season, and much more of this kind of weather would exact a costly toll. The ewes had come through poorly during the winter, and a weakened ewe usually meant a poor lamb. A bad winter usually caused a heavier predator toll, and this one was certainly bearing that out. Raising livestock of any kind was a hard business. A man had so many things to beat: the weather, the predators, the poisonous weeds, the assorted ailments that felled sheep. A sheep was the damnedest animal. For no particular reason, it could lay down and die. Even if there was a God, it was hard to assume that He was on a sheepman's side. Jessie wondered if such thoughts occurred to cattlemen. He supposed they had their own sources of grief. Jessie really didn't give a damn what happened to any cattlemen. They deserved everything bad that happened to them.

Jessie grinned faintly as he thought of the language his grandfather used whenever a cattleman was mentioned. Asa Kilmer was so badly crippled up that he could barely get around. That crippling could be directly attributed to the cattlemen, or a couple of them at least.

Jessie shook his head as he remembered how painfully Asa got around some mornings. Asa had lost his belief in a God many years ago, and Jessie could scarcely blame him. Asa ranted against God often enough. How many times had Jessie heard old Asa bellow, "Don't give me any more of that. If there was a Supreme Being sitting up there, do you think He would allow such suffering to go on in this world?" Asa didn't care who he flung those words at. Several times, Jessie had seen a preacher stamp out in affront from the house, vowing never to come back. That suited Asa just fine. The harder life grew, the more Jessie began to believe that Asa could probably be right. The first time he had arrived at that conclusion it had frightened him. He had looked fearfully at the sky, fully expecting to see a bolt of lightning hurled at him. But nothing had happened, and that helped him anchor more firmly his disbelief. As he grew into manhood, he had been able to see that Asa was right. There was nothing to look out for mankind but the individual himself. God certainly hadn't looked out for either cattlemen or sheepmen when the war between them had blown up. Jessie had been only a kid of ten years when the frightening news had spread through the countryside. The cattlemen were trying to run the sheepmen out of the country. Those had been bad days and fearful nights. There had been raids on animals and men, and if a woman got in the way, that was just tough on her. Jessie had attended many a funeral of some of the Kilmers' friends. The one he would remember forever was that of his father. He had stared long at the still form in the coffin. This wasn't the man he remembered; there was no laughter or humor in this grim form. He had remained at the coffin side until his mother seized his arm and pulled him away. Jessie had protested, saying, "This is the last time I'll ever see him."

She had looked at him, her eyes brimming with tears in a white, stark face. "I know, Jessie. But it won't do any good standing here."

The law had never been able to find the skulking killer who had loosened the murderous bullet from ambush. But Asa had his suspicions. "It was one of the damned Hagens," he had thundered. "Someday I'll—" He always left the threat unfinished. Perhaps, in his helplessness, he realized there was really nothing he could do.

Though it couldn't be proven, Jessie knew his father's death could be blamed on the cattlemen. If he had to pick out a name, he would choose the Hagens. Asa had harangued Quint Raines often on the matter, and each time Raines had shrugged and said, "Bring me some proof." Asa hadn't been able to do that. In an indirect way, the blame for the loss of Jessie's mother could be attributed to the same source. She hadn't lasted long after his father died. Daily, Jessie could see her fade away. He could remember Asa exhorting her that she had to eat something. She had stared at him with those sick eyes and quietly shaken her head. Then one morning, she hadn't awakened. A kid could know such tearing grief that it tore him apart. "Why did it have to happen, Grandpa?" he demanded.

Asa had shaken his head. "I wish I could tell you, son. But I can't. But believe me, someday we'll find a way to even up the score."

A new blast of wind raked Jessie, bringing him back to reality. He had to go around the corner ahead and get some sheep medicine. That would finish his shopping chore. He dreaded to turn the corner and face the blast of wind he knew would be there. The wind was strong down this street, and it always seemed to swirl at the corner ahead until a man felt as though the wind was taking him apart. We never evened the score, Grandpa, he thought. The war had died of its own weight, and the killing of people and the slaughtering of animals had slowly faded. Full credit could be given to Quint Raines. This was mostly cattle country, and there was little or no money to support what Raines had in mind. He had saved a little money, and by using it he had ignored the vise he had been in. He had hired a half-dozen tough men with guns, and he had let the county know what he had done. "I don't give a damn whether it's cattlemen or sheepmen." Jessie's lips twisted in a mirthless grin as he remembered how thoroughly Raines had kept that promise. It had taken killings on both sides; Raines's hired-gun help had collected cattlemen and sheepmen. If they got any segment of proof that anyone was involved, those deputies went out and gunned-down the offenders. How the cattle population of the county had screamed. They had vowed vengeance against Raines, and for a couple of elections it had looked as though they would make their vows come true. But the sheepmen had collected solidly behind Raines, and he had squeaked narrowly through two elections. Then men had become sickened of the slaughter, and slowly the heated tempers had cooled. Now, you couldn't find a cattleman against Raines. They learned that peace was far better than war. Now Raines was solidly in office. Raines couldn't teach the two factions to love each other. It would take years for men to learn even tolerance. But all agreed peace was better.

Men learned that cattle and sheep could live in the same county. All the cattlemen's belief that sheep would destroy the grass by eating it down to the roots was proven false. In fact, sheep manure was beneficial for the grass. It made it grow more luxuriant, turning its green so dark that it looked black. Education and Raines's stern hand had changed viewpoints, and the cattlemen had grumblingly accepted the enforced peace. That didn't mean the two factions had any liking for each other; they only had to accept what was inevitable.

This county owes Raines a big vote of thanks, Jessie thought, and ducked his head before he turned the corner.

Goddamned wind, he thought as the blast scoured him. It came so quickly and so fiercely that it sucked his breath away.

He didn't see Grat Hagen coming down the street toward him. If it had been possible, he would have avoided him. He didn't like a Hagen any more now than he had formerly.

"Hey," he heard somebody say in a startled voice. "Watch where you're going—"

The sentence was never finished. Jessie's bowed head plowed into Hagen's chest, and the impact jerked a startled ejaculation out of him. Jessie got a strong whiff of whiskey-laden breath, then the bulky figure was going down.

For an instant, Jessie thought he too was going to lose his footing. But with a nimble skipping and a swinging of his arms he held his balance. He didn't know who he had run into until he glanced at the prostrate figure.

He sucked in a harsh, tearing breath. Their animosity was ancient, and no apology or offer of assistance would ever enter his mind.

Hagen looked up at him with a passion-enflamed face. "Why, goddamn you," he said jerkily. "Why in the hell don't you watch where you're going?"

Jessie looked at that hated face with sardonic amusement. He couldn't remember a time when he hadn't disliked the Hagens, particularly Grat. It seemed as though they were fated to battle almost from the moment they had met. How well he remembered their first encounter. He hadn't been ten years old when Hagen had resented his talking to Beth Cagel. Jessie had been carrying her books to school, and Hagen had thrust out a sneaky foot, tripping him.

Hagen had laughed in uproarious delight, and that added to Jessie's embarrassment. Sure, he liked Beth. He had ever since he had met her. She was small and sweet with enormous, guileless, blue eyes. They went well with that shining mass of blond hair. Jessie wasn't old enough to be able to express what he felt. He just knew he liked her.

"You tripped me." He blurted out the accusation.

"Don't be blaming me for your clumsiness," Hagen denied the charge.

"I'll show you," Jessie howled, scrambling to his feet.

It had been quite a fight. Both boys were about equal in weight, and their skills were a match. Jessie was bleeding from the nose and lips, and his head rang. But he had marked Hagen as thoroughly. He didn't know how long it had lasted, but it seemed forever. His legs trembled, and his arms were so heavy he could scarcely keep them up. The first few minutes had taken some of the fierce determination out of both of them, and they came together, wrapping their arms about each other. They were so arm weary that they needed the support of each other upon which to lean. Jessie had gotten a foot behind Hagen's leg and jerked on it. They had gone down together, clawing and rolling on the ground. Jessie didn't know how much longer it would last, but he was getting awfully weary of this fight. Beth's screaming had brought all the other kids running up to form a shouting ring about the struggling combatants. The schoolteacher, hearing the commotion, came racing out and broke it up.

She berated both equally, then, when the first surge of her anger subsided, managed to say in a calmer tone, "Now, what's this all about? Who started this?"

"*He* did," Jessie shouted, pointing at Hagen. "He tripped me."

"He's a liar," Hagen said virtuously. "He's blaming his clumsiness on me."

The sheer effrontery of the lie wiped away Jessie's weariness, and he wanted to go at it again. In fact, he even started at Hagen, but the teacher was faster. She darted in between them and said with severity, "I think both of you are to blame. Both of you will stay after school. If there's any more of this disgraceful conduct, you'll stay after school every day until the end of the year."

Neither of them wanted to face such a frightening prospect. They sat across the room, staring straight ahead. Every now and then they stole a glowering glance at each other.

The teacher finally released them a couple of hours later. "Remember what I said," she warned. "If you get in more trouble, I'll hear about it. And I'll punish you."

Jessie would have given anything to get at Hagen again, but the teacher's threat rang loud in his head. By Hagen's menacing look, he suspected Hagen felt the same way. They parted without further entanglement.

That old scene flashed through Jessie's mind. He was more than willing to pick up the old quarrel. This time there was no one around to stop it.

"Why don't you get up, Grat?" he asked softly.

Hagen's face filled with red. "Don't think I won't," he roared. He put his hands against the street and lifted himself. Jessie let him have a moment to brush himself off. If Beth was here to watch this, it would be almost like the first time. He hadn't seen her for the past four years. Oh, that wasn't absolutely true, for he had seen her when she came home during the summer months. That damned eastern school had changed her. She wasn't at all like he remembered her.

He set himself to meet Hagen's rush. Hagen might deny this, but Jessie had the advantage. Hagen had been drinking; it showed in the shine of his eyes, and Jessie had smelled liquor on his breath at the moment of the first impact. Jessie was a ruggedly handsome man when he was smiling. Smiling was the last thing in his mind now. The old hatred had reflamed, and it was a roaring fire inside him. He had so many grudges to wipe away. "What's holding you back?" he taunted.

Hagen bellowed as though he had been kicked in a sensitive spot. He came with a rush.

Jessie ducked the first swing. Hagen was consumed with a rage too, for the swing had more power than finesse. The fist whistled over Jessie's head. He returned the blow, getting the solid weight of his shoulder behind his blow. It landed squarely in the middle of Hagen's face. It had power and resentment propelling it, and the impact knocked Hagen off his feet. He landed on his back, and he lay there gathering his scattered senses.

"If you think staying down will let you escape more of the same, you're wrong," Jessie taunted. "I can kick the hell out of you."

Maybe that wasn't too wise, for it pumped new energy into Hagen. "You sheepherding bastard," he roared. He got his muscles bunched under him, and he came off the street as though he had been catapulted through the air. But he had learned a little wisdom. He didn't try to regain his full height. He propelled his weight just below Jessie's waist, and his shoulders rammed into Jessie's thighs.

Jessie got just a glimpse of a blood-smeared face before his knees buckled under the enraged bulk. He went over, landing on his back. His head completed the arc, slamming into the hard street.

That set bells to ringing in Jessie's head, and his vision was impaired. For an instant the breath was knocked out of him, and it took a moment to regroup his senses. He kept blinking his eyes to clear them, and he saw that mocking face swirling above him.

"What's the matter, big mouth?" Hagen tormented him. "Do you think staying down there will save you the rest of your punishment? As you pointed out to me, I can kick the hell out of you."

That ground Jessie's teeth together. "Be right with you," he growled.

Jessie intended using the same tactics, to launch himself off the ground in a rush, a rush so great that it would overwhelm Hagen.

He had a headache, and his vision wasn't as clear as he wanted, but he would make it do. He came up in one quick motion, but Hagen was waiting for just such a move.

He retreated just enough that Jessie couldn't reach him in one motion. He lashed out with a savage boot, kicking high.

Jessie saw the kick coming, but he had already committed himself, and he couldn't alter his course. He threw up one arm in defense and pulled his head deep into his coat collar.

He saved most of the kick from landing, but there was still enough force to fill his head with angry clamoring, and furious, red stars floated before his eyes. He was going down again, and he couldn't do a thing to stop it.

From a far-off distance, he thought he vaguely heard a woman scream. It sounded familiar, but he couldn't place it.

"Stop it," the woman screamed. "Stop it, both of you."

Jessie lay in the street, trying to regain his scattered senses. That kick had only scraped the side of his jaw, and it left him weak and wobbly. The spot where the boot had scraped felt raw, and he lifted a weak hand and touched it. He had to focus his eyes to make out what they saw. The fingers were stained. He was bleeding. He didn't hear the woman's voice anymore. Maybe that was only a figment of his imagination.

"Goddamn you, Hagen," he said in a husky voice. "This isn't done yet."

"You Kilmers were always hardheaded," Hagen replied. "You never had enough sense to know when you were whipped."

Further talk was useless, Jessie thought. Words wouldn't whip Hagen. It was going to take pure muscle to close that boasting mouth. Strength was flowing back into Jessie. His only concern was that Hagen would try to finish the job by stomping him to pieces. He couldn't lay here and wait for that to happen.

Jessie threw himself to the left, rolling along the street. His movement caught Hagen by surprise. It showed in his startled ejaculation. "That won't do you any good," he shouted.

Jessie heard the heavy pound of Hagen's feet as he took after him. The only thing he could do was to keep on rolling until he figured he had enough space between them for him to attempt to get back on his feet.

CHAPTER 3

Beth Cagel didn't see Hagen kick Jessie. She had already whirled and was running down the street. Raines's office was a good block away, and she had to get him to break up the fight. Nobody else would be able to do it.

She was panting when she ran into Raines's office. He was slumped in his chair, his back toward her, but he heard the thud of her feet. He spun, and his face tightened at what he saw.

"Hey, now," he said gently. "What's got you so excited, Beth?"

"Quint, you've got to come right away. Jessie and Grat are fighting a block down the street."

That jerked Raines out of his chair. He was painfully thin, and that craggy face went with the rawhide body. He had spent a lot of years in this office, and it was beginning to show on him. "You're sure?" he barked.

She nodded, tight-lipped. "I saw it."

He strapped on his gun belt and reached for his hat. "What got them started?"

Beth didn't think she could control the tears much longer. She squinched her eyes fiercely. "I don't know. They were at it when I came up. Oh, please hurry, Quint."

"I'm hurrying," he said testily. He stormed out of the door with her at his heels. Oh God, he thought mournfully. Probably an aftermath of the old war. He had thought that was dead. He hastily corrected the thought. He had hoped it was dead. He guessed that once the seeds of hatred were planted in men's hearts, they never really died. All it needed was the feeblest of excuses to give it a new impetus. An open fight between two of the chief contenders could be the breath to send it into full flame.

He pounded down the street. A crowd had gathered around the two contestants, and the faint echoes of their encouragement carried to him. This could be it, he thought, his mouth open with his breathing. Most of those watchers were cattlemen. By numbers, this was still cattle country.

For a moment, the ring of onlookers kept him from seeing the contestants. Then the ring of watchers shifted before the motion of the battling men, and Raines caught sight of them.

Jessie was rolling about on the ground, and Hagen was rushing after him, trying to pin him down. It must have been a rough fight so far, for Jessie to be down like this.

Raines pumped new determination into his legs. These legs had seen too much service for him to put such demands on them, but he had to break this up before any more damage was done.

Jessie managed to make it to his feet before Raines reached the scene. For an instant, Raines had the impression that Jessie was trying to seek room in which to flee. He discarded that impression immediately. He didn't know what Jessie was trying to do, but he had never known of a Kilmer that ever had the smallest bit of run in him. Whatever Jessie had in mind, it certainly wasn't running.

Jessie made a quick dash to the perimeter of the crowd. He whirled there, and even at this distance Raines could see the fury on his bloody face.

Jessie planted himself and yelled, "Come on, you bastard."

Hagen came with a rush. His face was bloody too. Both the battlers had drawn blood.

Jessie stood his ground almost until Hagen reached him. He must have gauged the intervening distance between them well, for he barely slipped aside before Hagen swung at him.

Hagen tried to check his rush and correct his aim at the same time. It threw him off balance, and he took several corrective steps. The fist didn't even come close to Jessie.

Hagen, that's gonna cost you, Raines thought.

Jessie followed Hagen. He caught up with him and swung a hamlike fist. Hagen was turned away from him, and the fist caught him on the back of the neck.

Hagen made a sound that was half grunt, half pain. The blow was powerful, and he bent under it. The lower he bent, the more he lost his balance. He tried to correct his loss of balance with quick, mincing steps, but it was a losing battle. The lower his head came to the street, the greater was the pull of gravity. He went down hard, his face plowing into the dirt. Some of the former momentum was still with him, for it pulled him along several feet.

He had the vitality of an ox, for he quickly struggled to his knees.

The effort was a tremendous drain, and he hung there, struggling for a little more purpose.

Jessie came up behind him. He locked his hands together and raised them high above his head. He smashed them down on Hagen's unprotected head.

It was enough of a blow to fell a grizzly. Hagen buckled under it, and again his face hit the street.

Jessie stood over him, breathing hard. "Get up," he raged. "I want you to get up."

"Hold it," Raines roared. "Stop it right now."

He had a carrying voice, and even at that, Jessie was so enraged he didn't hear him.

Hagen's body straightened out, and an arm reached out as though the hand was trying to find something to grip and pull the body along. Then the hand flattened out limply, and there was no other motion in any other part of the body.

"I said, Get up," Jessie panted. He drew back a boot and kicked Hagen in the thigh. The kick had enough force to jolt Hagen forward a couple of feet.

Raines jerked out his gun, pointed it at the sky, and pulled the trigger a couple of times. "When I said, Stop it, I meant it."

The reports turned Jessie's head, and the belligerence on his face faded into a sheepish look. "Hello, Quint. I didn't know you were anywhere around."

"Evidently." Raines put his gun away. "It's a good thing Beth told me about this going on. Would you have tried to kick him to death, Jessie?"

Jessie got that hangdog look. "Aw, Quint," he said plaintively. "You know I wouldn't have done that."

"I know of no such a thing," Raines snapped. "You were sure trying to when I stopped it."

Jessie apparently saw Beth for the first time. "I didn't see you, Beth."

Her chin was too high to please him. Beth always looked like this when she was affronted. "That was apparent," she said icily. "Is that all you and Grat do, fight?"

Jessie winced. That schoolboy fight had evidently lodged in her mind. "You know it's not like that," he said quietly.

Her sniff showed her disbelief.

Jessie turned to Raines. He had incurred the displeasure of both of them. Of the two, Raines was the worst, for Raines could hurt him.

"I owed Grat that, Quint," Jessie said slowly. "He tried to kick my head off. Look at my face." He knew it was still bleeding, for he could feel the moistness there. "Do you think I was going to let him get away with that?"

Raines inspected the bruised and bleeding area. "I guess not," he said grudgingly.

"Oh, Jessie," Beth cried. "You're bleeding."

That gave him a little hope. She was displeased with him, but not so much as not to be concerned over him.

"Who started this brawl?" Raines demanded.

"I guess I did," Jessie admitted. "Both of us came around the corner at the same time. I didn't see him, and I doubt he saw me. The impact knocked him down. I tried to apologize, but words couldn't reach him. All he wanted was fight. He was drunk, Quint. I smelled it on his breath."

"Sure it wasn't the memory of the old war driving both of you?" Raines asked.

"That never entered my mind," Jessie said evenly. "I admit I didn't have any use for him. The damned Hagens caused the Kilmers enough trouble."

Raines's sigh was heavy with defeat. "I suppose the Kilmers were blameless in any way. It'll never end, will it? I was hoping you people would get a little sense in your heads. That doesn't look like it's ever going to happen. I'm arresting both of you."

"What for?" Jessie yelped. "Are you saying a man hasn't the right to protect himself?"

Raines glared at him. "You know better than that. This wasn't a simple case of self-protection. I'm arresting both of you for disturbing the peace."

"How long are you going to hold us?" Jessie demanded.

"Overnight at least. I'll let the judge decide in the morning what to do with you."

"I've got to get back," Jessie said in quick protest. "If I don't, that leaves old Asa alone. You know he can't get around very well."

Raines shook his head. "Are you trying to tell me there's nobody else out at the place?"

Jessie gave up in defeat. Raines was too smart for that excuse to work. The Kilmers hired a dozen men the year around. There would be someone to look after Asa, and Raines knew it. "Come on. Let's get this over," Jessie growled.

Raines grinned. "Thought you'd see it my way." He looked around at the crowd. "A couple of you help Hagen to his feet and bring him to jail."

Raines was a hard-eyed man. If either of the two he selected had any intention of refusing his order, it faded quickly under that steely gaze.

Hagen was just coming to as they bent over him. He groaned and swore and even fought the hands trying to help him.

Raines moved over to where Hagen lay and snapped, "Grat, you cut out that damned nonsense, or I'll make it a lot tougher on you."

Hagen tried to meet Raines's eyes and failed. "Where are you taking me?" he asked sullenly.

"I thought you'd have figured that out by now," Raines said sardonically. "You're going to jail for disturbing the peace."

"You can't do that to me," Hagen howled. "Put the blame where it should be. That damned Kilmer started it all. He walked into me."

Raines looked over his shoulder and saw the red flood over Jessie's face. "That's enough of that," he barked. "I'll be the judge of who's to be arrested. I don't want to hear another word out of you."

He moved back to Jessie and said, "Start walking." He glanced at Beth, who was still there. "You'd better come along too, Beth."

"She had nothing to do with this," Jessie yelped. "You can't arrest her."

Raines's eyes filled with exasperation. "Why in the hell don't you find out what's going on before you make a judgment? I want to find out how much she knows about this."

"She doesn't know anything," Jessie said stubbornly. "She wasn't even here when it started."

"Do you mind going, Beth?" Raines asked.

"I don't mind, but I don't know much, Sheriff."

Raines took her elbow. "I'd appreciate it, Beth."

Jessie took the lead, followed by Hagen and the two men who were helping him. Raines and Beth brought up the rear. By the time they reached the sheriff's office, Hagen was moving fairly well.

"That's enough," Raines said, taking over. "I can handle it from here on." He looked at the crowd that had followed the small procession. "Break it up," he shouted. "There's nothing more to see."

"You oughta hang that damned sheepherder," somebody in the crowd shouted. "They've always made the trouble."

Raines seemed to grow a couple of inches taller. "That's enough of that kind of talk," he said, his voice edged. "My God, I thought all of you could remember the bad days of the war. Or has it slipped completely from your minds? Do you want to see the bloodshed come back again?"

Somebody in the crowd hooted at him, and the jeering was picked up and swelled. Raines stared them down until the hooting died. A man turned and walked away. He was followed by a couple more, then the entire crowd was dispersing.

Raines was tight-lipped as he closed and locked the door. He looked at Hagen and Jessie with disgust. "You heard it. Is that what you hoped to bring back?"

"Hell, it wasn't my fault," Hagen said defiantly.

Jessie hung his head. At least, he had enough sensitivity to have some feeling.

Raines picked up a ring of keys from its peg. "Come on," he said, his voice tight. "I'm locking you up in separate cells. I don't want to hear a damned word out of either of you."

Jessie paused before he entered the corridor between the cells. "Beth," he said reproachfully. "I didn't think you'd do this."

Raines's shove propelled him forward. He came back, and Beth was still standing. "Sit down, Beth," he said, his voice softening.

"What's going to happen to them?" she asked, her voice concerned.

"Not enough, I'm afraid," Raines answered. "Probably a small fine. I wish the judge would lock them up until some sense was pounded into their hard heads."

Beth shook her head, but she remained silent. She kept twisting at the fingers of a glove.

"Do you know what started it, Beth?"

There was distress in her eyes as she stared at him. "They were fighting when I came up. I screamed at them to stop it. But if they heard me, neither of them acted like it."

"This wasn't the first time they've fought," Raines said grimly.

Beth didn't know he referred to the war. "No," she agreed. "They fought once while all of us were just kids. Grat tripped Jessie while he was carrying my school books." Her eyes clouded at the memory. "That was an awful fight. I don't know what would have happened if the teacher hadn't stopped it."

Raines looked at her with renewed interest. "I didn't know their bad feeling started that far back." He rapped his knuckles against his desk in quick irritation. "When a man gets filled with hatred, nothing seems to dissolve it."

"I don't remember the bad days too well," Beth said. "Shortly after it started, my father sent me away to school. I didn't go through the war. Oh, I came back during the summers. I heard enough to know that it was pretty bad. You stopped that war, didn't you, Quint?"

"I never put out the fire," Raines growled. "It's still smoldering."

"And you're afraid it'll start up again?" Beth asked in quick perception.

"Exactly. Just a spark catching in the wrong place, and the whole thing could go up again. What just happened could be that spark." He sat there in moody silence, staring at his desk.

He looked up at Beth. "Were you and Jessie close? I mean in the early days." He didn't miss a small spot of color appearing in her cheeks.

"It meant nothing, Sheriff. Jessie and I quarreled before I left for school. That wiped out all prior feelings."

She still feels something, Raines thought. It still shows. "I'm not trying to pry into your personal life, Beth," he apologized. He raised a hand to pacify her.

She shrugged irritably. "It doesn't matter." A little temper showed in her tone. "Why do you ask?"

"I was just wondering if you had any influence left with Jessie. Maybe a few words coming from you would do a lot of good."

The flush deepened in her cheeks. "Nothing I could say would mean a thing to him, Quint."

Ah, Raines thought. She's too much on the defensive.

Beth stood. "Is that all?"

Raines gulped. "One other thing. I'm afraid I have to ask you to appear at the trial in the morning."

A flash of temper appeared in her eyes. "I won't do it," she said heatedly.

"Your testimony would be important, Beth. You saw the start of the fight. The judge will be interested in your telling of the earlier fight between them."

Her back was too straight. "Suppose I refuse?" she said coldly.

Raines sighed. These soft-appearing women could be tough. "Then I'd have to issue a warrant for you to appear in court. I hope you don't make me do that."

She sucked in a deep breath, hollowing her cheeks. "I guess there's nothing to do but to obey."

Raines blew out a long breath. "I appreciate your cooperation, Beth."

Her shrug was supposed to show her indifference.

Raines never took his eyes off her as she left his office. His eyes were shadowed.

He wasn't indulging in idle talk when he said the whole county could blow up again. As close as he kept an eye on things, he was surprised to find how thin the temper was today. There was that fight between Jessie and Grat, there were the remarks of the crowd. It seemed as though the hotheads were only eagerly waiting for something to show them the way.

He listened incredulously. The voices were coming from the cells behind his office, and at first he couldn't make out what they were saying.

His face congested with wrath as he caught a few words. It was Jessie and Hagen, jawing at each other. They larded every remark they made at each other with plenty of cuss words.

"Stop it," he yelled. "Or I'll come back there and shut you up."

He scowled at the following silence. His authority still held. You'd think locking them up would have put a subduing clamp on them. It hadn't. My God! How deep that hatred went. It scared Raines just to think of its intensity.

CHAPTER 4

Keeley felt drained as he watched Raines take Kilmer and Hagen away. His eyes were shining, and he kept licking his lips.

He didn't know Benson was anywhere near until Benson spoke. "Jesus Christ," Benson said in an awed voice. "I thought Jessie was going to kill him until Raines broke it up."

"A hell of a battle," Keeley agreed absently.

"They've hated each other for a long time," Benson said sagely. "Ever since the sheep/cattle war."

Keeley's mind kept picking at something that he couldn't quite sort out. It was a shame all that hatred was being used to no avail. It was too bad a man couldn't put it to use.

A thought ran through his head like a bolt of lightning. He was aquiver with an inner excitement. Maybe this was what he had been looking for, for such a long time.

"Benson, don't we have a loan on the Kilmers' property?"

"You should know," Benson said reproachfully. "You okayed a granting of it shortly after your father died."

Keeley remembered now. In the onslaught of everything he had to do at his father's death, he had put the loan aside in his mind. But maybe now was the proper time to review it.

"Charley, get me the papers on that loan. I'd like to look it over."

Benson hid his nod of approval. Maybe Jacob was beginning to take an interest in the running of this business.

Benson brought the papers in to Keeley in his office. He lingered, an expectant look on his face.

"That's all," Keeley said, annoyed. He knew what Benson expected. He wanted to stand there ready to answer any and all questions about the Kilmer loan. Keeley didn't need him. He wasn't sure what he was going to do with this loan. He only wanted to thumb through it again in case an opportunity came up.

He settled back in his chair and looked at the first page. The Kilmers had a nice piece of property. Of course, the eight thousand acres wasn't nearly as big as some of the cattle spreads, but if Keeley had his hands on it, it would do nicely. His eyes gleamed as he thought of how much the Kilmer land would bring at a forced sale.

The deeper he got into the papers, the more absorbed his face became. It wasn't a big loan at first. Jessie had made the first year's payment. But he had increased the loan during the second period. These figures suggested that the Kilmers were having a rough time making that piece of land pay.

Jessie had made the payment the second year barely beating the due date. If a man was doing well, he didn't put off the important chore of keeping his loan paid up. If he missed that date, he could be facing a foreclosure.

Keeley finished going through the papers. He tilted back his head and stared at the ceiling. All that information was locked in his head. Just let Jessie miss the payment coming up in May, and the Kilmers would lose their land.

Keeley sighed regretfully. He was glad he had gone through the loan papers, though he still didn't see what he could do about it. How was he going to make Jessie miss the next payment? Keeley searched his mind and didn't come up with a thing. He wished the Hagens were still engaged in open warfare with the Kilmers. That would certainly disrupt the Kilmers' shipping schedule, and that would throttle their cash flow. Without that flow of cash, there would be no money to make a payment. Without that payment, Keeley would have a valuable piece of property.

"Oh, damn it," Keeley said aloud. He had all the tools to make a dream work. The trouble was that he didn't dare do anything about it. He wasn't a physical man, and he shuddered at just the thought of going up against Jessie. He wished there was someone he could hire to make it impossible for the Kilmers to make any money. He ran through a mental list of names of men who might be capable of doing what he wanted. Oh, he could pay them, but that wasn't the problem. They would be afraid of Quint Raines; they wouldn't dare arouse his wrath.

Keeley tapped his teeth with a forefinger. He would bet he could hire a dozen cattlemen to do what he wanted. But the amount of money wouldn't be enough to allay their fears of Raines. The sigh came from the pit of Keeley's belly. It was a beautiful dream, and he had everything to make it work except for one glaring lack. He couldn't think of a single man, or several, to give the idea impetus.

He put all the papers in their folder and bellowed, "Charley."

Benson came in, his eyes apprehensive. Keeley thought he always looked this way whenever he was summoned in here.

"Yes, sir?"

"Put the folder away," Keeley ordered. "Make a mental note of the due date. If Jessie misses it by as much as an hour, I want to be informed. Do you understand me?"

"He won't miss," Benson was emboldened enough to say. "That property means too much to him. Old Asa Kilmer first settled on it. He and his son added a little more land to the original amount. No, Jessie would never risk losing it."

"I didn't ask for a history of the Kilmer family," Keeley said coldly. "I asked you to put this folder back. Is that too hard to understand?"

Old Benson gulped and seemed to shrivel. He lived in mortal fear of offending Jacob Keeley. "No, sir." He picked up the folder and hurried out of the office.

Keeley frowned at the closed door. Benson was typical of the kind of tools he had to use in accomplishing a job; weak and ineffectual, breaking under the first pressure. He would be of absolutely no use in driving the Kilmers to a point where they lost their property. But this idea was something to keep alive in his mind. Something might come up. He had a little time before that payment came due.

Keeley left the bank at four o'clock. He shivered as the wind wrapped around him. Why would anybody willingly pick such a miserable country to live in? Now and then a passerby nodded to him. It wasn't that way when his father was alive. Old Cyrus knew everybody in town and the surrounding country. Everybody seemed anxious to keep on good terms with him. Now Jacob was treated almost as an outsider.

To hell with all of them, he thought in sudden rage. He didn't have to live in this town, and he wasn't going to. He was going to get out of it just as fast as he could. He thought longingly again of the Kilmer property. If that was his to sell, it would bring in a magnificent sum, enough for him to be able to live how and where he pleased. That old longing for Cynthia filled his being again. He wasn't going to give up on her. He still had time.

He made his way to where he lived and stared with disfavor at the faded old house. It had been in the Keeley hands for three generations. Cyrus thought of it as a wonderful house. Jacob could remember him talking about it until he wanted to scream.

Old Mrs. Larson met him in the doorway and assisted him off

with his coat. "Supper will be ready in thirty minutes," she said crisply.

Keeley didn't care much for her, though she did her work efficiently, and she was a passable cook. He could hire her cheaply, and that was consideration enough. Rarely was there communication between them, and he didn't try to break the dour silence that mostly surrounded her. She had nothing to say that would interest him, and he was quite sure she wouldn't be interested in his world.

"That'll be fine, Mrs. Larson," Keeley responded. He faced another one of the same humdrum meals. Mrs. Larson wasn't an imaginative cook. She used a fry pan too often, and at times she served the same meal several times running. It wasn't that way in San Francisco. His belly twisted at the memory of some of the meals he had had there.

CHAPTER 5

Raines finished serving breakfast to the two cells. Jessie took a sip of his coffee and grimaced. It was worse than awful.

Hagen, in the next cell, reacted with more violence. He flung the cup of coffee across the cell, the cup clattered against the bars, the liquid splashing out into the corridor. "Goddamn stuff ain't fit to slop hogs with," Hagen raved.

Raines had just turned away. He whirled, his cheeks burning. "Grat, I'd say you'd make a fit judge of that," he snapped.

"What's that supposed to mean?" Hagen growled.

"I'll put it so plain even *you* can understand." The rancor was pronounced in Raines's voice. "Ain't nobody more fit to know what a hog wouldn't like."

Hagen rushed to the bars, gripping them with such intensity that his knuckles stood out starkly. "That goddamn badge don't give you any right to insult me."

"Then don't make remarks that invite them," Raines said unfeelingly. "I've got to clean up the mess you made." He started to turn away, then changed his mind and paused. "If you don't want your breakfast, just don't eat it. But don't try throwing it around."

"You must already know it's bad," Hagen sneered.

Raines locked eyes with Hagen until Hagen gave way. "Just because you got me locked up don't mean you got any right to treat me like an animal," Hagen said sullenly.

"Then quit acting like one. You better clean up a little. You're going up before a judge in a couple of hours."

That drew surprise from Hagen, and he howled indignantly. "Why should I face a judge? All I did was try to defend myself."

"Why don't you stop that?" Raines asked wearily. "Do you want a lawyer? You've got enough time to hire one."

"I don't need no lawyer." The sullenness was more pronounced in Hagen's voice.

Raines shrugged. "Suit yourself."

Raines moved on to Jessie's cell. "Did you hear that conversation?"

Jessie grinned. "I couldn't miss it, could I? If you want an opinion to back you up, I'm afraid I'll have to agree with Grat. It was god-awful coffee."

"You're a real funny man," Raines said sourly. "Do you want a lawyer?"

Worry touched Jessie's face. "Do you think I need one?"

"You'll be going up before Judge Manning. He heard a lot of the cases during the cattleman/sheepman war. He got a full belly of the arguments from both sides. He worked his butt off, and he's never forgotten it. He wouldn't want to go through that again. He feels like I do. Stamp out any spark before it spreads into a roaring fire. I'm afraid he won't be sympathetic to either of you."

"You sound like you think I'll need a lawyer."

"You might," Raines said cautiously. He stared in amazement as Jessie shook his head. "You don't agree with me?"

"I don't know," Jessie said miserably. "I'm thinking of a lawyer's fee. There'll be a fine, won't there?"

"You can depend on it," Raines said crisply.

"Then a lawyer's fee will just be more expense on top of the fine. I'll just have to take my chances."

"You're running your own show," Raines said and stalked away.

Jessie moved closer to the wall that separated his and Hagen's cell. "Grat," he called. "Did you hear that?"

"So what?" Hagen answered surlily.

"Both of us could be facing a fine," Jessie said.

"You could be," Hagen snapped. "You ran into me. You threw the first punch. If the judge finds any guilt, it'll be yours, not mine."

"Why, you miserable bastard." Jessie managed to catch his temper before it fully exploded. "I hope you get what you deserve."

He turned away and flung himself on his bunk. His face was set hard against Hagen's jeering laughter. Those Hagens were always hardheaded.

Raines came back before ten o'clock. "We've just got about enough time to get over to the courthouse. Let's go."

He unlocked both cells. He looked at the emerging prisoners and shook his head. "If you two ain't the most impressive sight."

"I couldn't do any better," Jessie said mockingly. "Your facilities ain't the best."

"We don't get the best trade," Raines said and grinned. His face sobered, and he said crisply, "I don't expect a minute of trouble out of either of you. If there's any, it'll only be added to your bill. That's big enough now."

He let the two precede him, and not a word was exchanged all the way to the courthouse.

Jessie couldn't help the little shiver running through him. This was a grim-looking building, and he wished desperately he was anywhere else but here. He had never been in here before, and he vowed this would be the last time.

Only a handful of spectators were in the courtroom. This wasn't a big enough case to draw the curiosity-seekers. His eyes widened as he saw Beth sitting in the first row. She had never forgiven him for that ancient quarrel, and she was here to see him squirm. He could think of no other reason. He took his eyes off her. This was a bleak room, and the chairs were hard. Only a few minutes of sitting in one put an ache in Jessie's butt, and he squirmed.

"I'd be squirming too if I faced what you do," Hagen whispered. Maybe he purposely didn't try to keep his voice low, for it had a carrying power. It reached the bailiff standing near the judge's bench, for he whipped his head about and scowled at Hagen.

Jessie's cheeks burned at Hagen's implication that only Jessie was guilty.

Raines frowned fiercely at both of them. "You two keep still," he hissed. "Unless you want to make the charges worse. Judge Manning don't stand for any disrespect in his courtroom."

Jessie looked down at his clasped hands. That big-mouthed Hagen wasn't going to be able to drag another remark out of him.

Judge Manning came in five minutes later. He was a dumpy figure with a full-moon face, almost ludicrous in appearance. But he was no laughing matter. He was a hard and decisive judge, and his punishment was quick and severe.

"Everybody stand," the bailiff intoned. "The court is in session, The Honorable Peter Manning presiding." He waited until Manning arranged the dingy, faintly green robe about him and settled down. "Everybody sit," he ordered.

Manning raked the two culprits with those fiery eyes, glanced at the papers before him, then said, "I see we haven't a very filled docket this morning, Bailiff."

The bailiff nodded. "No, sir. It's a light day."

Manning was a testy man. "Well, get on with it."

Oh Lord, Jessie thought. He sounds mad before he hears a word. That little shiver of apprehension ran through him again.

"Grat Hagen and Jessie Kilmer arraigned on a charge of fighting and disturbing the peace," the bailiff said.

Those busy eyebrows rose, and those terrible eyes surveyed Jessie and Hagen. "Have they been here before?"

"I don't think so, sir. The names sound familiar because their families have been in here before, but that was quite a few years back. That was in the time of the cattle/sheep war."

"Some more of that," Manning said frostily. "Are they back at that again? Who is the arresting officer?"

Raines stood and said, "I am, sir. Sheriff Quint Raines."

Manning didn't look at Raines with much favor. This man had brought him a lot of trouble. "Get on with it, Sheriff."

"Yes, sir. I came up while they were fighting. These two never had much love for each other."

"I'll be the judge of that," Manning snapped.

Raines's appearance didn't change much, though his lips thinned. He drew in a deep breath and said, "It was almost over when I arrived. Hagen was out cold. Kilmer kicked Hagen just as I came up."

Hagen bounded to his feet, his face impassioned. "He ran into me, then hit me," he bellowed. "Ain't that enough reason for me to try and get back at him?"

Manning pounded furiously with his gavel, and his face turned a shade of purple. "Sit down, Mr. Hagen," he said in icy tones. "You'll get your chance to speak. But only when I ask for it. Is that understood?"

The pounding didn't stop until Hagen resumed his chair.

Oh God, Jessie mourned. He's tough this morning. He's going to go hard against both of us.

"Go on, Sheriff," Manning ordered.

"They were coming in opposite directions. They turned a corner and collided. I guess there were a few hot words, though I didn't hear them. Kilmer lost his temper and busted Hagen in the nose. Hagen spilled into Kilmer and knocked Kilmer down. When Kilmer attempted to get up, Hagen tried to kick his head off. Your Honor can see the marks of that kick on Kilmer's face."

Those glacial eyes surveyed Jessie's damage, then the judge asked, "Is there more?"

"Not much. Kilmer knocked him out. He kicked him just as I came up. I got what information I have from a witness."

"Is that witness here?"

"Yes, sir. A lady. Miss Beth Cagel."

Manning's face softened as Beth stood. Very few males could

remain tough under those appealing eyes. "Come forward, Miss Cagel. There's nothing to be frightened of."

The bailiff swore Beth in, and Manning said, "Tell us exactly what you saw."

"I didn't see the start. They were fighting when I came up. I screamed at them to stop, but if they heard, it made no difference. I went after Sheriff Raines. It went just as Sheriff Raines told you." A shiver of apprehension ran through her.

"Did the fight frighten you that much?" Manning asked curiously.

"I guess it did, sir. It wasn't the first time I'd seen them fighting."

"Ah," Manning said, his eyes lighting with interest. "When did that first fight occur?"

She gestured helplessly. "Years ago. We were just kids. Jessie was carrying my school books. Grat tripped him. They tore at each other with the same ferocity. Only the teacher coming out stopped it."

"So there's been no love lost between them?"

"I guess not," Beth said helplessly.

Manning leaned forward, and his face was tense. "Sheriff, do you think this could be another outbreak of the old trouble?"

"I don't think so, sir. I think it was just an accident. Hagen had been drinking. I smelled it on his breath as I locked him up. I thought I'd better bring them up and let you talk to them. I knew you'd want to squash it before it spread any farther."

"Wise," Manning granted. "Mr. Kilmer, will you approach the bench?"

Jessie's knees were shaking as he got to his feet. That dumpy little man behind the bench couldn't do anything to physically hurt him. An adverse little opinion jeered in his mind. The hell he can't. He can make it so rough you'll wish you'd never been born.

"Tell your side of it, Mr. Kilmer."

"I ran into Grat. I came around a corner and the wind was blowing so hard that I tucked my chin into my collar. I know I should have been watching where I was going. I tried to apologize, but Grat was all het up. He wouldn't listen. I guess the liquor he'd drunk pushed him on."

"You're positive he was drinking?"

"I smelled it, sir."

That satisfied Manning, for he nodded. "Go on."

"He said something I couldn't take. I hit him and knocked him down. He went wild. He dove into me without fully getting to his feet. It spilled me over. When I tried to get up, he tried to kick me in the face. I saw it coming in time to pull my head to one side. But his boot scraped my jaw." He canted his head to one side, so that the judge could get an unobstructed view of the damage.

He couldn't tell anything by the judge's nod. That might have been in sympathy or total indifference.

"I knocked him out, sir. I hurt, and I guess I lost my head. I was so mad I kicked him in the leg. Quint must have come up then. He fired a couple of times in the air to stop me."

"You were resisting an officer of the law?" Manning sounded appalled.

Jessie looked pained. "Good Lord no, sir. I didn't even know he was around until I heard the shots. I wouldn't refuse to do anything Quint told me to do."

"That'll do," Manning said, tight-lipped. "Mr. Hagen."

Jessie went back to his chair, and Hagen approached the bench.

"I want to hear your side of the story," Manning said. He sounded like a big tomcat making a hungry sound before he sprang. "Had you been drinking?"

Hagen twisted and jerked as though he was trying to escape a patch of quicksand.

Jessie watched with great interest. Would Hagen lie or admit the truth?

Hagen caved in before the merciless onslaught of Manning's scrutiny.

"I'd had a couple of drinks, Your Honor," he mumbled. "It was a cold day. I was just trying to fortify myself against the wind. I was minding my own business when this clumsy clown ran me down. Sure, it made me hot. Wouldn't you be mad if somebody knocked you down?"

"I'm not involved in this, Mr. Hagen." Manning's voice was colder than a day in deep winter. "Go on."

"I got up and took after him. I knocked him down, but he managed to get back on his feet. He sneaked in a lucky punch. That's all I remember."

"You left out the part about kicking at Mr. Kilmer."

"He's also a liar," Hagen protested.

"How do you think he got that bad bruise on his jaw?"

"I wouldn't know," Hagen said heatedly. "I've told you how clumsy he is."

"I don't believe any part of your story, Mr. Hagen. You've had a hatred for the Kilmers for a long time. They're sheepmen, and your family tried to run them out of the country. Sheriff Raines stopped that, and I'm here to see that it doesn't happen again." Manning's voice picked up a thundering note. "Do you realize that just this little incident could have reopened all the old hatreds? Sheriff Raines said a number of the spectators were heavily in favor of your efforts. That fight could have been the spark igniting the tinder pile. I will not have that sad, dreary business starting again. I find you guilty. The fine will be one hundred dollars. If something like this ever occurs again, I'll see that a stiff jail sentence goes with it. I advise you not to even look cross-eyed at a Kilmer."

"That's not fair," Hagen yelped. "I didn't start it."

"But you didn't try to avoid it, either. The fine is still one hundred dollars. Either pay it, or go to jail for sixty days."

"I'll pay it," Hagen said in a surly voice. He pulled a wad of bills out of his pocket and thumbed off several of them.

"Pay the clerk," Manning said, and for the first time today he sounded almost happy. "I advise you to keep what I said in mind, Mr. Hagen. If you don't, you'll find they weren't just empty words."

Hagen glanced at Jessie before he left. He had more poison in his eyes than a rattlesnake.

"Mr. Kilmer," Manning called.

Jessie shook. Now it was his turn. He had no doubt his punishment would be fully as severe as Hagen's. He approached the bench and said weakly, "Yes, sir."

"Did you listen to what I told Mr. Hagen?"

Jessie nodded.

"Good. Then I won't have to repeat it. The same fine goes for you. Avoid a Hagen like the plague. If you tangle with one of them again, you'll think this morning's punishment was only a mild form of child's play. Do you understand me?"

Jessie gulped and nodded. The amount of the fine made him pale. Money hadn't been in plentiful supply around the Kilmer place. The last two years they hadn't even made expenses. He didn't have anywhere near a hundred dollars in his pocket.

"Well?" Manning asked impatiently.

"I haven't got the fine, sir," Jessie said frantically.

"Then you'll be locked up until your family raises it," Manning answered implacably. "It's your choice. What is it?"

Jessie didn't move. He stood there, wrestling with an almost insurmountable problem.

"Sheriff," Manning said. "Take this man back and lock him up. He will be held until his fine is met, or sixty days."

Jessie knew the amount of his account in Keeley's bank. It barely reached over a hundred dollars. He wasn't being given a decision to make. He was being forced into it.

"Sir," he said hoarsely, "I can get the amount you request out of the bank. Could I have permission to go get it?"

Manning gave him that ice-tipped grin. "I think it's a wise decision, Mr. Kilmer. Sheriff, go with him to the bank. When he has the required amount, bring him back so that he can pay the clerk."

Raines walked out of the courtroom with Jessie. On the way across the street he kept glancing at Jessie. "The judge made it tough, Jessie?"

"Damned tough," Jessie said despondently. "It about strips us to the bone."

Raines shook his head. "Don't come down on the judge too hard, Jessie. He went through hell during the war. He's got a good memory. I don't blame him for not wanting to go back into that time again."

"That goddamned Hagen," Jessie burst out.

Raines shook his head in disapproval. "He wasn't alone, Jessie. The two of you made a pair. Get that attitude out of your system. It'll eat you up. As long as you're steeped in hatred, one wrong word, a sour glance can touch you off again."

"You mean I should accept anything he wants to hand me?"

"I don't think that will happen, Jessie. Not after this session. I sympathize with you because of the bind it puts you in. It's a hard lesson, but maybe it's an effective one."

He stopped just inside the bank and let Jessie go on to the cage alone.

Keeley was in the cage. Jessie had never really liked the man. He was so damned cold and withdrawn.

"How'd you bruise your face, Jessie?" Keeley couldn't quite hide the false ring in his voice.

"I was learning something," Jessie said bitterly. "I'd like to make a withdrawal of a hundred dollars."

Keeley frowned to hide the gleam in his eyes. "That won't leave you very much."

"I know how much I've got left," Jessie said shortly. He handed over his passbook.

Keeley made a notation in it, then handed the passbook and two fifty-dollar bills back to Jessie. "I hope you have a good reason to use this money."

"Maybe not a good one," Jessie said hollowly. "But a very compelling one."

He rejoined Raines. "I'm all ready to close out this little deal."

"Sure," Raines said laconically.

CHAPTER 6

Jessie's unhappiness didn't lessen as he paid the livery-stable bill. Instead of an expected fifty-cent fee, it was a dollar and a half, the charge for an all-night rental and two feedings.

"Expected you back yesterday afternoon," Hank, the owner of the stable, said.

"Something happened to tie me up," Jessie said shortly. It wasn't Hank's fault, but Jessie was at loggerheads with the world. That goddamned Hagen. Of all the people he might have run into turning the corner, it had to be him.

He mounted, nodded abruptly to Hank, and set out for home. He had less than a couple of dollars in his pocket, and he didn't dare dwell on how the amount in the bank had dwindled. He didn't dare think too much about telling Asa about this. The size of the fine would put a strain in Asa's face. Jessie wouldn't blame him if he cussed him out good. That would be another aftermath of what happened when a man lost his temper. It not only hurt him, it hurt everyone closely associated with him.

He rode onto Kilmer land, and up ahead of him was a blatting flock of sheep. Deke Cummings ambled along behind them. Deke had been with the Kilmers longer than Jessie could clearly remember. He was bent, his straggly hair was white, and his face was lined. He had no other ambition than to shepherd sheep. His old legs were getting tired, but he could still cover his six miles a day. Jessie had speculated often upon what Deke would do when there was no more go left in those legs. A man who couldn't get around couldn't make much of a shepherd. Though Deke had never said anything, Jessie imagined Deke had worried about the same thing. Jessie shuddered. It must be horrible to face the inevitable and be unable to do anything about it. Counting Deke and Asa, this was getting to be an outfit of cripples.

Jessie pulled up beside Deke. "Think it's a little early to be taking the sheep out, Deke?"

Deke flashed him a grin with several gaps in it. "Howdy, Jessie. Asa didn't think so. He said there might be a mouthful of grass in some sheltered places."

There was no arguing with that. Asa was a sheepman and had been all his life. He thought like a sheep, and he had an instinct for what was best for them.

Jessie gave in. "Well, if Asa thinks it's all right."

Deke gummed his cud of tobacco, then spat an amber stream to the ground. "It'll do them good. They've been penned up for so long they're getting restless. They're sick and tired of hay. Besides, every mouthful they pick up will save our dwindling hay."

"Don't wear yourself out," Jessie warned.

"I know of some land that's sheltered on three sides by rises. I'm hopeful to find a little grass there." He cocked a curious eye at Jessie. "Asa was worried when you didn't come in last night." He cackled and slapped his thigh. "I told him there was no need to. The blood starts rising in a young buck about this time of the year. I told Asa you'd probably stopped at one of the houses in Landers."

Jessie laughed shortly as he felt his cheeks heating up. He wished he had spent the night in one of Landers' infamous houses rather than where he did.

"Not that," he denied. "Something came up that I couldn't avoid." Again, he repeated his warning. "Don't go too far. That wind still has a bite in it."

He nodded and put his horse into motion. He rode carefully around the small flock Deke was driving. They didn't look too bad, he thought, after looking them over critically. He would have liked to have seen more meat on them, but that would come in a hurry, once the grass started.

He dismounted and put the bay in the horse barn. He scooped up a measure of oats from the bin and scowled at the level of the grain. They wouldn't get through to grass time without having to replenish their oat supply. He resisted the urge to curse at the way things mounted up on a man once things started going downhill. That hundred dollars would have bought a lot of oats.

He walked into the house, and Asa was limping about the stove. He couldn't get around very well without the aid of a cane. Often he cussed that game leg, but he refused to give up. Jessie could remember when he was a kid how Asa could keep up with anybody. That had changed in a hurry after his accident.

Asa turned a craggy face toward Jessie as he came in. Those features had turned into leather. That happened when a man had spent as much time in Wyoming weather as Asa had.

"Thought you'd forgotten where you lived," he said sourly.

"You weren't worried about me?" Jessie asked in pretended surprise.

"Hell, no. I figured you were old enough to take care of yourself."

Jessie gulped. He might as well tell Asa where he'd been, but the words stuck in his throat. "I couldn't make it, Grandpa," he said without looking at Asa.

"Was she that good?" Asa asked. "Deke said you stopped over in some house."

Jessie still couldn't look at him. "It wasn't a woman, Grandpa."

Asa's eyes sharpened. "Then what in the hell held you up?"

Jessie's throat felt tight. He had never lied to Asa, and he wasn't about to start now. "I was in jail, Grandpa."

Asa's jaw sagged, and he laid down his mixing bowl. "In jail? What the hell for?"

Jessie busied himself hanging up his hat and sheepskin. "I got in a fight."

"A fight?" Asa ejaculated. "It must have been a hell of a fight to get you jailed."

"It was a pretty good one," Jessie said carefully. "Quint arrested me."

"Since when is a fight grounds for arresting a man?" Asa asked sarcastically.

"I guess it kinda depends upon who the fight was with."

"Who was it with?"

"Grat Hagen." Jessie's throat felt dry.

"Hagen," Asa exploded. "Boy, turn around and look at me. You've got a lot of talking to do."

Jessie faced him. "My head was down to avoid the wind. I turned a corner and ran into him. He said a few things I didn't like, and I busted him in the nose."

"Good for you," Asa said with enthusiasm.

Asa's ebullience wouldn't be so high when Jessie told him the rest of this.

"I wish you'd have broken his goddamned neck," Asa said heatedly. "I'll never get over blaming the Hagens for this leg."

Jessie nodded. That was almost beyond a doubt, though it hadn't been proven legally. The Hagens were responsible for the accident. It was the Hagens' cattle that were involved, but a clever lawyer had gotten them off in court. Nobody had seen the cattle driven over Asa and his horse and the flock of sheep he was herding. Asa testified that he'd heard gunshots, and shortly after that, the cattle had swept down over him. He had been completely unprepared for it. The rush of the cattle had carried Asa and his horse over a bluff, the horse landing on him. It was a minor miracle he hadn't been killed. When he was discovered, he was unconscious. The leg had been badly shattered. They had gotten him to a doctor in town, and the doctor had wanted to take the leg off. Asa had refused. He had come into the world in one piece; he was going out the same way. For a couple of weeks everybody thought he was going to do just that. Infection had set in, and only Jessie's father's stubborn refusal had prevented the doctor from amputating the leg. Then the tide turned, and slowly Asa mended. All but the leg. It would never be the same. That bad leg had chained him to the house or close to it. He couldn't herd sheep, help in the shearing, or do anything that a normal, active man could do. Riding was completely out of the question.

"I hope you kicked the hell out of that Hagen," Asa said furiously.

"I tried to," Jessie said with a bleak grin. "That's when Quint came up. I had a good enough reason. Grat tried to kick my head off." He turned his head so that Asa could see the bruise on his jaw.

"Why, that low-lifed bastard," Asa exploded.

"I got back on my feet and knocked him cold," Jessie said simply. "It made me so mad that when he couldn't get up, I kicked him in the leg."

"He had it coming," Asa said savagely.

"Quint didn't approve as much as you do. He arrested both of us and held us for trial in the morning."

"He arrested you for just fighting?" Asa fumed.

"It was more than that," Jessie said slowly. "It was just a small replay of the old war. Quint jawed us good how much it had cost him to stop the original one. He wasn't going to have another one started."

"I don't believe this," Asa said incredulously. "If some damned cattleman insults you, you can't do anything about it."

"Something like that," Jessie admitted. "Judge Manning belabored us on the same subject. Listening to him and Quint, you would think a new war was ready to break out."

Asa's face was getting redder. "Old Judge Manning?"

Jessie nodded. "The same."

"He and Quint stopped the first war," Asa said. "In fact, he listened to my case against the Hagens. I'll never forget his decision. There wasn't enough proof for him to come to a conclusion. Why, damn him?" he said wrathfully. "I had this busted leg, didn't I?"

Jessie couldn't answer that question. He had been too young to attend the hearing. "From what I hear, he's always been fair."

"Fair, hell," Asa stormed. "Did he find that Hagen was guilty?"

"He found both of us guilty. He fined the two of us."

Asa stared as though he was hearing blasphemy. His face purpled, and he sounded as though he was choking. "Both of you? Why, goddamn it, he can't do that."

"He did," Jessie said grimly. He dreaded the next question. He might as well answer it before Asa got it out. "He fined each of us a hundred dollars. I had to draw a hundred dollars out of the bank."

"God Almighty," Asa screamed. "There ain't no justice in this damned country anymore."

Jessie had no intention of arguing that with Asa, particularly when he was in this mood. "Grandpa, it cut us way down." He winced as he thought of the few dollars left in the account. "I had to pay it, or spend sixty days in jail."

"Did that old fool threaten that worthless Hagen with the same thing?"

"Grat had enough money on him to pay the fine." Jessie's eyes were shadowed as he recalled that courtroom scene. "The judge lectured me pretty good. He was sick and tired of the fighting between cattlemen and sheepmen. He warned me if I fought with another cattleman I'd do a stretch of time. He meant it."

"What do you do if some damned cattleman comes up and spits in your face?"

Jessie grinned painfully. "Ignore it and go on. I'm not even to look cross-eyed at one of them."

Asa choked until he was breathless. He sputtered and managed to say faintly, "I can't believe it."

"Believe it. It happened. I'm not worried about that. I can avoid cattlemen. I'm worried about our bank account. It's down next to nothing. We've got a payment to make come May. If we can't make it, you know what can happen."

That put Asa into a deep study. He had carved this piece of land out of a wilderness. He had fought for this land, and that included against the Indians. Land hadn't been very valuable in those days. But it was now. By God, nobody was going to take it away from them.

"Something will turn up, Jessie. We'll make a big shipment of lambs before that payment is due. Ain't nobody going to get their hands on our land."

Jessie sighed. "I pray to God you're right, Grandpa." As for himself, he couldn't help but be dubious. The winter had been severe. The loss had been high. The ewes hadn't come through the winter in the best of condition. That could mean a poor lambing season. Jessie couldn't see where they were going to get a lamb crop to make that shipment. It was a rough life, one strain after another.

"It'll turn out all right, son. It always has before. I better get busy getting supper ready."

"Not much," Jessie replied. "I'm not very hungry."

CHAPTER 7

Keeley was stiff with resentment as he said good night to Benson and left the bank. Another dreary evening lay ahead of him. He would go home, eat a monotonous meal, read the pitiful little paper that was supposed to furnish the town news, then go to bed. It would be just like all the dreary days that trudged by in dull procession. If he had a big enough piece of land, he would sell out, then hurry to San Francisco. A piece such as the Kilmers owned, he thought once again. For the past few days he had thought of nothing else. The opportunity dangled before his eyes, blinding him. All he had to do was reach out and pluck that opportunity. There would never be a better time. The Kilmers were desperately short of money. All they had to do was to miss the May payment, and that piece of land would be his. It would probably happen, but how could he be sure? The Kilmers might have some assets he didn't know of. He wanted to throw back his head and howl in frustration.

He nodded curtly to a couple of passersby. Neither of them could tell anything by his impassive face. God, how he hated this little town and all its people.

He plodded on to his house, pausing a moment to rake it with resentful eyes. He was chained here, for how long he didn't know.

Mrs. Larson met him at the door. She took his hat and coat. Something had happened to brighten her day; it showed in the shine in her eyes.

"Jacob, there's a man waiting to see you. He says he's an old friend. Will he be staying for supper?"

The vibrance in her voice said she hoped so. Anything to break the usual routine.

"Didn't he give his name?" Keeley asked sharply.

She shook her head. "He didn't. He said you'd know him well enough. Shall I set another plate at the table?"

"Not until I know who he is," Keeley answered acidly. Right now this man was a total stranger. Keeley had no intention of furnishing a meal to a stranger.

He paused and drew a deep breath before he opened the parlor door. The room was semidark, for Mrs. Larson didn't believe in leaving the shades up. Sunlight faded the upholstery and the carpet. Besides, the room was rarely used.

Keeley opened the door. Whoever this man was, he'd get rid of him in a hurry.

The man sat with his back toward the door, and for a moment Keeley didn't recognize him. He got the impression of utter weariness, for the big frame was sagging. From what little he could see of his clothes, he would say the man was in bad financial shape. The clothes were worn to the point of shabbiness.

The sound of Keeley's entrance caught the man's attention, and he slowly stood and turned. "Hello, Jacob," he said softly.

Keeley's mouth sagged open. It had been over five years since he had seen his brother. Curt Keeley was some six years older than Jacob, and Jacob used to adore him. That was before he got in trouble with the law. Cyrus had turned his back on his oldest son, for he was a man of high moral principles. Curt had thrown in with bank robbers, and that was even a greater insult to Cyrus. Curt and his small gang had been caught just as they came out of a bank. There was no doubt they were guilty. Each of them had a money sack in his hand. Thank God, it had happened in another town. The old man hadn't even attempted to attend Curt's trial. As far as he was concerned, Curt no longer lived. He had suffered under the humility of his son being a bank robber, and Jacob remembered well how he had raved and ranted about the crime. "Forget him, Jacob," Cyrus had shouted at him. "From now on, consider him as dead."

At first it was hard to do, but time healed the sense of loss. In the last three years he hadn't thought of Curt until this moment.

Keeley grabbed the back of a chair for support. "Hello, Curt," he said in an emotionless voice.

"Surprised to see me, Jacob?"

"Shouldn't I be?" Keeley answered flatly.

"Still unforgiving, huh, Jacob? I committed a crime. I was drunk and too young to think straight. We talked over a robbery that night, and by morning I was so drunk I fell in with the plan. I served my five years. I guess Father never forgave me."

"You should know that," Keeley said unmoved.

"It rubbed off on you well," Curt said reflectively.

"Why did you come here?" Keeley asked angrily.

Curt winced and rubbed a hand over his eyes. "I didn't have anyplace else to go, Jacob."

"You wouldn't have come here if Father was alive."

Curt smiled painfully. "You're right about that, Jacob. Father was an unforgiving man. I was hoping you'd been cast in a different mold."

"State what you want." The anger was still in Keeley's voice.

"I'm broke, Jacob." Curt patted a pocket as though to emphasize its emptiness. "Maybe I was hoping you'd see a way to help me. Five years taught me my lesson. I'd never do anything that could get me sent back again."

"Do you see any reason why I should help you?" Keeley asked stiffly.

Curt stared at him a long moment. "Still unbending, aren't you, Jacob? The old man shaped you well." For a moment, his face was sad, then it turned stern. "Forget I was ever here. I've got a room paid up for a few days. I'll get by."

He started for the door, and Keeley moved to block his passage. All the memories of a happier childhood flooded up in Keeley, softening him.

He reached into his pocket and pulled out a few bills. He shuffled through them until he picked out a twenty. He handed it to Curt and said, "Maybe this will help some."

For a moment, he was sure Curt would refuse the offer. Then Curt shrugged and grasped the bill. "My thanks."

Keeley was certain there was a mocking note in Curt's voice. "Where are you staying?" He caught the resentment in Curt's eyes and added hastily, "In case I want to get in touch with you."

"At the Drovers' Hotel," Curt said, his voice stiff.

Keeley managed to hide his grimace. That was nothing but a flea trap. It had only one advantage. It was cheap. "This is no promise, Curt, but I may want to see you later."

Curt nodded. "It's not like the old days, is it?"

Again, the old memories flooded back, and Keeley felt a constriction in his throat. His face flamed, but he managed to keep a curb on his tongue. He wasn't responsible for the predicament Curt was in.

He stood aside for Curt to pass. Curt searched his face, then shrugged before he left. Keeley could only be grateful that Curt didn't try to shake hands or utter anything maudlin.

Keeley couldn't get to sleep that night. He rolled and tossed, then suddenly sat upright. The solution to the problem that was deviling him was right before his eyes. All he had to do was get Curt to agree to it. His face set in bleak lines. Curt might refuse to listen to him. Keeley shook a clenched fist. Curt had to. There was no other way out for him. Keeley would see Curt the first thing in the morning.

It was surprising how quickly sleep came after he reached that decision. San Francisco wasn't nearly as far away as he thought it was.

Keeley scowled as he stood out in front of the Drovers' Hotel. Curt must really be at the end of his rope to be forced to live in a hole like this. He shook his head against any weakness that might flood over him. He didn't come down here to commiserate with Curt; he came down to show him how to get out of the deep hole he was in.

The hotel looked bad on the outside, but stepping into the dingy small lobby, it looked even worse. The lobby was dirty, and the smell was offensive. Strips of old paint hung from the ceiling, and the walls were scabrous. What few pieces of furniture there were in the lobby were a disgrace. The upholstery was faded until it was almost impossible to determine the original color. Some of the upholstery was split, and the stuffing showed through.

God, Keeley thought, what a hole. He shuddered inwardly at the thought of having to live in a place like this.

He advanced to the desk, and an old man dozed there. He wasn't old, Keeley amended. He was ancient. He looked around for a bell, and there wasn't one. He'd have to awaken the desk clerk to get an answer to a question.

"Hey," he called. With no response, he repeated the word, raising his voice. After the fourth fruitless attempt, Keeley's patience wore thin. He reached across the desk, seized the bony shoulder, and shook him vigorously.

Rheumy old eyes flew open, and the clerk stared vaguely at Keeley. "What's the matter?" he mumbled. He looked reproachfully at Keeley. "Shouldn't have waked me up," he mumbled.

"I had to, to get an answer to a question," Keeley said in disgust.

The sunken old cheeks flushed. "If you're saying I sleep too much, you're wrong. I just happened to doze off. There wasn't much to do this morning. I ain't no charitable case. I get my room and a couple of dollars a week."

"Magnificent wages," Keeley jeered. He wanted to say, You're probably not worth that much, but held the words. "Do you have a

Curt Keeley registered?" He had to repeat the question before he could make the old man understand.

The old man rose, and Keeley could swear his joints creaked and groaned. "Believe I do," he mumbled. "Let me see." He studied an ancient ledger while Keeley waited impatiently. He wanted to get out of this place as quickly as he could.

"Yep," the old man said in elation. "There he is. Thought I remembered that name. Room one ten. What do you want to see him about?"

"That's none of your business," Keeley said crisply. He turned away from the desk. He hadn't gone two paces before he heard the clerk mutter, "One of those damned stuckup rich men. He don't give a damn about poor people."

Keeley grinned bleakly. He cared about poor people. Wasn't he here to lift one of them out of his misery?

The smell grew worse as he moved down the hall, looking at the numbers on the doors. He was mildly surprised that the doors still had numbers. With each step that musty, dusty smell strengthened. He could swear this place hadn't been cleaned in years. Cobwebs festooned the walls. He paused before room 110. His repugnance was noticeable. Maybe this wasn't such a wise idea, coming here.

He raised his knuckles and rapped vigorously. His rage mounted at the lack of response. Was everybody in this place deaf? He knocked again, his knuckles making the door resound.

"Yes?" he heard a sleep-fogged voice reply. "What is it?"

"Curt, it's Jacob. I want to see you."

Curt was taking forever to open the door, and Keeley's temper rose. The inclination to turn away from this door grew stronger. In fact, he was on the verge of leaving when he heard the scratching of a key, and the door opened.

Curt stood there, his eyes speculative. He had taken time to put on his pants and shirt, though he was barefooted. "Didn't expect to see you here, Jacob."

"When I talked to you I didn't expect to be here," Keeley snapped. "Can I come in?"

"Sure," Curt answered laconically. He stepped aside for Jacob to enter and said apologetically, "Isn't much, is it?"

"I'm surprised this place even has a key to a lock," Keeley said waspishly.

Curt flushed, but he held his temper. "A man has to do with what's handed him."

The only items in the room were a chair and a bed. Curt had

some articles of his clothing on the chair. He cleared it off, then waved a hand at it. "Go ahead. Sit down."

Keeley was seething at himself for being here, and at Curt for checking in at such a miserable hotel. He couldn't find a logical place to start, and he turned words over in his mind.

Curt sat on the edge of the bed, and he shifted a couple of times. "Why don't you just say what's on your mind, Jacob?"

Keeley coughed. "Your predicament bothered me," he said haltingly. "I couldn't get to sleep last night. Then an idea of how to help you came to me."

"I wouldn't want to put you to too much trouble," Curt murmured.

Keeley looked sharply at him. Was that mockery he caught? He decided he was too sensitive, and the words began to flow. "Would ten thousand dollars set you up?"

Curt stared at him with opaque eyes. "You, a banker, offering me that kind of a loan. I can't believe it."

"It's not a loan," Keeley said harshly. "It's payment for a service you could do for me."

"It must be a pretty dangerous service to offer that kind of money."

"Not *that* dangerous," Keeley corrected. "If you use your head, there's hardly any danger at all."

Curt pursed his lips. "Then it's illegal. I told you I'd never do anything that could get me sent back."

Keeley made a chopping motion with his hand, dismissing Curt's words. "If you don't want it—" He let the words trail off.

"I didn't say that," Curt objected. "You haven't told me yet what you want done."

Keeley drew in a deep breath. Now he had to put it into plain words, and the thought scared him. "There's a piece of land I want. I already have a loan on it. If the payment coming due is missed, I can foreclose on that land."

"Ah," Curt said knowingly. A streak of cheat lay in his beloved brother. "You want me to kill the landowner so that payment can't be made."

"No, no," Keeley said hurriedly. "I just want his shipping schedule so messed up that he can't possibly sell enough stock to get the money he needs."

Curt sat there for so long, his gaze remote and faraway, that it scared Keeley. Curt wasn't going to do it.

"What kind of stock?" Curt asked.

"He owns sheep," Keeley answered.

"Does he have sheepherders around him?"

"Yes, but they won't cause you any problems. Every sheepherder I've known has been on the old and helpless side."

Curt pulled at his fingers, making a popping sound. "But what if the sheepherders step in the way and do cause trouble?"

"Then remove him," Keeley said bleakly.

"It's a big job for a single man," Curt mused.

"The offer's big enough," Keeley countered. "Don't you know of someone you could get?"

For the first time, Curt met his brother's eyes directly. "I know of two boys who did time with me. I imagine they'll be interested. They're probably having the same trouble as I am."

Ah, Keeley thought exultantly. He is thinking about doing it. "Yes?" he asked anxiously.

"When would I get the ten thousand dollars?"

"I'd pay you right away."

Curt's eyebrows rose. "Before the work is completed? What's to keep me from stuffing the money into my pocket and leaving the country?"

"That would force me to turn you over to the law. With your record, I don't think it would take much to convince the law that you're at it again."

A wince momentarily twisted Curt's face. "You'd do it too, wouldn't you?"

"I would, if you tried to cross me. All you have to do is deliver. The money is all yours without any questions asked."

Curt sat there in an agony of indecision. He looked at Keeley, and there was a new toughness in his face. "I don't know what you're going to do with the land. But maybe this will be a mutual benefit to the Keeley brothers. When will you have the money here?"

"I'll have it here in the morning," Keeley answered. He thought of a few more words to ease Curt. "The law would never be looking for you." He briefly told Curt of the old hatred between cattlemen and sheepmen. "It's broken out again. If the law becomes involved, they'd be looking for cattlemen." He stood and crossed to the door. He stopped there for a final warning. "Play this straight, Curt, or you'll have the law on your tail. I don't think anything would be worth going back to the place where you spent five pleasant years." He laughed sardonically at the bleakness that washed across Curt's face.

CHAPTER 8

Keeley was back at Curt's hotel in the morning. The desk clerk was asleep again, and Keeley didn't bother to stop by his desk. He knocked on the door of room 110, and this time Curt was awake, for he answered immediately. He let Keeley in, and his eyes were veiled. "Good morning, Jacob."

Keeley was in a better mood than he had been in recent days. Ten thousand dollars, even in sizable bills, made a comfortable bulge in his pocket. He had entered the withdrawal in the ledger as a loan he had personally made. The name to whom the loan was made was fictitious. Benson would never question anything Keeley did. The only danger of discovery would be if the bank examiners made a surprise visit. But that wasn't likely. They had inspected the bank a little less than a month ago. He had every reason to be in high good spirits. He had set the wheels in motion, the wheels that would get him out of Landers and on to San Francisco.

"Did you contact the others?" Keeley asked, sitting down.

"I sent Young and Royal a wire yesterday," Curt replied. "They haven't replied yet."

"They might not be interested," Keeley said, his anxiety showing.

Curt laughed with no humor. If Young and Royal had found the going as difficult as he had, there wouldn't be a doubt that they'd be interested. An ex-con found it hard to keep body and soul together. There wasn't much charity in men for one who had made a serious slip. He laughed again, a brief burst of jarring sound. "I expect to hear from them sometime today. They'll be interested all right." In his wire he had offered them a job that would be profitable.

Keeley reached into his breast pocket and pulled out the packet of bills. He didn't miss the gleam in Curt's eyes as he saw the money. He tossed the packet over to Curt, who caught it deftly.

"Aren't you going to count it?" he asked as Curt tucked it away in a pocket.

Curt grinned, a flash of wolf fangs. "If I can't trust you, then there isn't anybody in the world I can trust."

Keeley didn't know whether that was faint praise or sarcasm. "It's all there, Curt. At the risk of sounding repetitious, I'm warning you not to try to just leave. I promise you law officers will be on the lookout for you."

A gleam of resentment shone briefly in Curt's eyes. "You've made that plain enough," he said stiffly. "After my experience, I wouldn't be foolish enough to risk being sent back."

Keeley's threat was futile, but Curt didn't know that. Keeley couldn't risk having anyone know about the ten thousand dollars. A sense of exultation spread through him. Things were going in his favor. The right man had stumbled into his hands, and that one's needs were so great that he couldn't do anything but follow Keeley's instructions.

For a long moment the silence was unbroken, each man wrapped up in his own thoughts. Keeley almost chuckled as he thought, Each would give a lot to know what the other was thinking.

Curt broke the silence. "You better fill me in about this place. I don't even know the owner's name."

"Kilmer," Keeley replied shortly. "It's owned by an old man, so crippled he can't get around. The one you'll have to worry about is Jessie Kilmer. A grandson. He's tough." He thought briefly of the fight he had witnessed. "Jessie's the only one who could cause you any trouble. The rest of the help is mostly older men, barely able to herd sheep."

"Sounds better all the time," Curt commented. He kept his voice flat. "Where is this land?"

"About fifteen miles out of town. Take the main road going east. You can't miss it. The house and outbuildings aren't much. I'd advise you not to go straight up to the house."

Curt grinned twistedly. "I'm not that reckless. Just what am I supposed to do?"

"The lambing season is almost upon us," Keeley answered. "Do anything that disrupts that lambing. I don't want the Kilmers having any lambs to ship." His flash of teeth was a parody of a grin. "Without that shipment, there's no way the Kilmers can meet that payment."

Curt nodded slowly. "You have any ideas how I can do that?"

"That's entirely up to you," Keeley answered savagely. "Sheep are stupid animals, easily disturbed. They go crazy if anything strange happens to them."

"Won't the herders protect them?"

"All they can," Keeley replied. "Why?"

"I was wondering how far you'd want me to go, if some herder got in the way."

"That's up to you, Curt. It all depends upon how much you want to keep that money."

Curt patted his pocket. "I want to keep it." What might happen to a sheepherder was of no concern to him. When a man had been up against it as tough as he had been for a prolonged period, his finest regard for others had been rubbed so raw that he no longer had any gloss on that regard.

Keeley stood, and his brother asked, "Do you want me to report to you?"

Keeley pondered that question, then shook his head. "I don't think it's necessary. It won't be wise for us to be seen together."

For an instant, Curt's face went rigid. Jacob couldn't make it any plainer that he didn't want to see him. He forced himself to relax. Maybe Jacob's handling was for the best. Curt didn't need anybody pointing out to him that what he was involved in was illegal. All he wanted to do was to get this job over in a hurry, then get out of this country as fast as possible.

"So long, Jacob," he murmured.

"Yes," Keeley returned.

Having this much money in his possession made Curt nervous. He couldn't deposit it in a bank. He could only depend upon himself for the money's safety. He did go out and buy a secondhand gun. The bluing was worn off, showing the gun had seen much service. But it seemed to be in excellent shape.

"I've tried it out. It shoots true," the store owner said.

"I'm going to take your word for that," Curt said easily. "If you misrepresented the gun in any way, I'll be back."

The implied threat didn't faze the store owner. "I'd expect you to do just that," he said frankly.

Curt got the gun, holster and belt for thirty-five dollars. The store-keeper threw in a box of shells. He seemed in high spirits as he completed the transaction. "You'll find it'll do anything you want it to do," he said.

"I hope you're right," Curt said dryly. He had picked out the smallest bill from the pack Jacob had given him. He had some change coming out of that, and it would take care of his expenses for several days. He took his purchases back to his hotel room. Now he had to wait until he heard from Young and Royal. While he waited, he had acquired protection of a rough sort for the money.

He counted off two thousand dollars and stuffed them into his pocket. He prowled the room, looking for a hiding place for the remaining money. A board gave a little under his tread, and he kept coming back to it. The end of the board was loose. Each time he put weight on it, then stepped off, the board seemed to spring back. The two nailheads were protruding from the board end, and each time he stepped on the board it seemed to make them more loose. He kneeled beside the board, pulled out a jackknife, and opened its heaviest blade.

He pried on the nails, getting the edge of the knife under the nailheads. He didn't dare use too much pressure for fear of snapping off the blade. The nails finally came out with a dismal thud.

Curt was breathing hard by the time he had the end of the board completely free. He bent the board back as far as he could without risking breaking it. Ah, he thought in pleasure. He couldn't want a more obscure hiding place than the small cavity beneath the board.

He deposited the money beneath the board, then replaced it in its former position. He had saved the nails he had extracted, and by using the heel of his boot, he pounded them back in. He pounded hard on them, not worrying about somebody hearing him in this miserable place. In the several days he had spent here, he had only noticed a few people.

He walked back and forth across the end of the board, and the board seemed more secure than it had before. His hard pounding must have found a new bite for the nails. He nodded in satisfaction. He could leave the room without worry for his secreted hoard.

The waiting could be tedious, but he could stand it.

At the end of three more days, he heard an almost apologetic knock on the door. He didn't know which one it was, but he could bet it was either Royal or Young. The knock had that furtive little sound.

He opened the door and said, "Jim Young. I was beginning to fear you hadn't got my wire."

Young was a small man with a closed, drawn face. Prison had taken a lot of the spirit out of him. He kept licking his lips and staring furtively about the room, as though in fear that somebody would spring out at him.

"Looking for a guard, Jim?" Curt taunted him.

"These days a man doesn't know what can happen," Young muttered.

"Hear anything about Royal?"

Young shook his head. "I haven't seen him since the day we got out of prison. I expected to see him here. I hope what you wired is true. It took the last of my money to take the stage here. What's so big?"

"Do you need money, Young?"

"I've forgotten what it looks like," Young growled. "Nobody wants to hire an ex-con."

"Maybe things will change." Curt shook his head. "I don't want to tell it twice. We'll wait until Royal gets here. Could you stand something to eat?"

"I've almost forgotten what that is too," Young said despondently.

"I'll pay for this meal."

Young ate wolfishly. The man was hungry. Curt kept staring at him with disbelieving eyes. Who would have thought it possible that a man could change so much? Before prison, Young was a fun-loving man, always on the lookout for a laugh. Young didn't know what Curt had in mind, but Curt didn't think there could be a possible refusal from him. Young had known bad times too long to make him refuse anything that might get him out of the rough days.

Rush Royal came in two days later. He was a big man, towering several inches over Curt. Curt couldn't see his face too plainly, for he had grown a full beard. He didn't think prison had changed him as much as it had Young. Royal wrung Curt's hand hard and said, "Good to see you again." He looked around the room, disfavor in his eyes. "I don't have to ask you how things are going. As bad as for me, or you'd have picked a better place to live. My God, what a dump."

"It's cheap."

"If they gave you this room for nothing, they'd still be robbing you."

Curt grinned. "Leaves a bad taste in your mouth, doesn't it? Want something to remove that bad taste?"

"I could sure use it," Royal growled.

Curt produced a bottle he had bought yesterday. He had three glasses to go with it. He poured them full and raised his glass. "Here's to better days."

"I sure hope they'll be better than some of the last five years we spent," Royal said savagely.

Young's wince was comment enough.

Royal tasted his drink and smacked his lips. "Damned good liquor. I can taste you haven't been doing too bad."

"What would you say if I told you I'd run across something that guarantees better times for all of us?"

"I'd say you're either drunk or just plain crazy," Royal grunted. "I know you haven't got a job. Our reputations slammed the door on that."

"This doesn't require us getting a job. We make our own jobs and get paid for it too." Curt drained his glass before he reached into his pocket and pulled out the money. How he enjoyed seeing two pairs of eyes bug out.

He counted two one-thousand-dollar piles, doing it with a flair. "Do you still think I'm crazy, Royal?"

Royal's face was tight with anticipation. "One of these piles supposed to be mine?"

Curt nodded. "It is."

Royal picked up one of the piles, and his fingers were almost caressing as he stroked the money. Young was more cautious in reaching for the remaining pile.

"There's gotta be a catch in this somewhere," Royal said suspiciously.

"There's a story behind it, Royal, but not a catch. Were you around here when war broke out between cattlemen and sheepmen?"

Royal shook his head. "I heard something about it, but I wasn't around." His eyes were watchful as he waited for Curt to go on.

Curt filled his glass again. He took a sip before he resumed. "A bad time. Quite a few men died and lots of animals. The law finally got enough help to squash it, but they couldn't squash the hatred. It remains until this day between the two factions. I'd say the cattlemen hate better than the sheepmen. That's who is paying us. They want a sheep operation stamped on." The story was entirely plausible, and he was satisfied.

"Hey," Young squalled, "that could get us in a heap of trouble."

Curt nodded. "If we're caught. But we won't be if we use our heads."

Royal was looking at him so oddly that Curt asked, "What's chewing on you?"

"I think you got more money out of this than you're giving us."

That annoyed Curt, and it showed in his face and words. "What if I am? I should be getting more. I'm setting everything up." He reached out his hand. "I thought I was doing you a favor. If you don't want that thousand, hand it back."

Royal pulled away, protecting the money he had thrust in his pocket. "I didn't say that, did I? I'm going along."

"How about you, Young?" Curt challenged.

Young was scared. It showed in his eyes and subdued manner. "If this blows up in our faces, we take all the brunt. The person who's hiring all this help won't be touched. If only I could be guaranteed there'd be no trouble—" His voice trailed away.

"When did you ever get a guarantee about anything in life?" Royal sneered. "You're not even guaranteed tomorrow." Young still fidgeted, and Royal said impatiently, "In or out? Make up your mind. Maybe Curt and I can do it alone. Just hand Curt back your money."

That prospect ground Young down. He knew from experience how hard it was to get his hands on a sizable chunk of money. "What are we supposed to do?" he whimpered.

"The sheepman we're supposed to hit first is short of money," Curt replied. "We're to disrupt his usual routine. Cut down his chances of getting a lamb crop. If we do it right, that'll run him out of the country."

"He's got sheepherders, ain't he?" Young demanded.

"Have you ever seen sheepherders? Most of them are old, helpless men. They won't be any problem."

"Yes, but they'll protect those sheep, won't they?"

"You're still after that guarantee, aren't you?" Royal sneered. "Are you going to let a few old men stop us from getting this money?"

Young's eyes shifted from face to face. "I guess not," he said unhappily. He struggled to make a decision, and the working of his face told how much spiritual agony it was costing him. "Hey," he said, as though discovering an alarming fact. "Even those old men will have rifles or guns to protect their flocks from wolves or coyotes."

"Probably," Curt said carelessly. "I'll buy some guns for both of you."

"When?" Young demanded.

"How about right now?" Curt had a momentary unease about having Young in on this. He had no such qualms about Royal. Royal was tough-fibered. He could be depended upon all the way through. He wasn't so sure about Young. Young had a basic weakness that might split wide open and hurt both of them. No, he decided. It wouldn't be that way. Young knew what he was facing in life. Curt was offering him the only way out.

As they left the hotel, Curt said, "You two can get rooms here. It's cheap."

Royal looked disgruntledly at the old relic.

"Not many people live here," Curt said sharply. "Do you want a bunch of people around you?"

"I guess not," Royal muttered.

"After a few days we won't be living here. We'll have things to do in the country that'll keep us busy."

He took the two to the sleazy little store where he had purchased his gun. "He'll sell us anything we want."

Royal viewed the store with growing disfavor. "I'll say one thing. You sure don't go first-class."

"Were you doing better?" Curt asked heatedly. Royal's remark had nettled him.

He walked inside, and the fat storekeeper waddled out to greet them. His greeting was jovial enough, but there was a small worry in his eyes. A former customer had returned and brought two hard cases with him. Did he have a complaint to make?

Curt's words dispelled his concern. "I liked what I bought from you so much I brought you two more customers."

The man became all affability. He dry-washed his hands and said, "Fine, fine. I'm sure I can suit you."

He showed what he had, and Royal and Young bought two handguns.

"We'll need rifles, too," Curt said. "We're planning on going on a little hunting trip."

Derision gleamed in the storekeeper's eyes. The gleam said, Hunting trip, hell. Well, it was none of his business. "What kind of rifles do you want?"

"Winchesters," Curt said promptly. A man could never go wrong on a Winchester.

"I never thought when I first saw you that you'd become one of the best customers I ever had," the fat man said.

"Keep that in mind," Curt said. "Maybe it'll help you knock something off the final bill."

"I'll make it rock-bottom," the fat man said solemnly.

Curt bought the five guns for a little over a hundred and fifty dollars. This thing was costing him more than he expected. He was going to have to purchase camping supplies and food. Maybe he should have demanded more from Jacob. It was something to keep in mind.

After this was all done, maybe he could come back at his brother and hit him for more.

After they left the store, Royal commented on Curt's free-spending. He cocked an eye at Curt. "I'd like to know how much you're getting for this. I've got a hunch it's a pretty sum."

"Don't fret about it," Curt said sharply. "I paid you what I offered." He knew one thing for certain. He was going to be alone when he bought the camping supplies. He groaned at the thought of another expense; he had to buy three horses, yes, and he would need a pack animal. He knew damned well he was going to come back at Jacob again.

CHAPTER 9

Asa tried to put more flapjacks on Jessie's plate, and Jessie howled his refusal. "My God, Asa, I've eaten eight already. You're either trying to kill me or make me fat."

There was no real censure in the words. Asa was better than a fair hand with a frying pan.

Asa grinned fiendishly. "I got an idea last night. If I could fatten you up, I might send you to the market. If I could get a fair price per pound, I might be able to turn a fair amount."

Jessie thought of the way he had spent a badly needed hundred dollars, and his face fell. "I wouldn't blame you. That would be one way to come out on me."

Asa limped over to the table and brandished the frying pan. "I don't want to hear any more of that kind of talk," he said fiercely. "You hear me? I'll knock some sense into that thick head. We've been in holes before. We'll get out of this one."

Jessie grinned sheepishly. Asa was a good man to be around. There was never a bit of give in him. "I didn't sleep very well last night," Jessie admitted. "I got to worrying about that money I spent foolishly."

"It's done," Asa said practically. "Forget it. Sure that was the real reason you couldn't sleep?" he asked slyly.

Jessie stared at him wide-eyed. "You'll have to say it plainer. I don't know what you mean."

Asa chortled, and his eyes danced. "Sure you weren't thinking about Beth? I'll bet she's been on your mind ever since you saw her."

Jessie scowled. "She has not," he denied. "I haven't thought of her since that quarrel."

"Was the quarrel the real reason you two broke up? Seems to me you were reaching kinda far when you demanded that she not go away to school."

Jessie's face turned brick-red. "That wasn't the real reason, though I let you think so. She was seeing Grat Hagen. I guess I really blew up." That wasn't really true. Beth had gone once with Hagen to a dance. Jessie had exploded when he heard about it. "I ordered her not to see Grat again," Jessie said miserably. "I guess that did it. It also helped her make up her mind about going away to school. I guess I was wrong."

Asa's mouth flew open. "You guess," he said incredulously. "That's the first time I heard about that phase. It'll do it every time. Nothing makes a high-spirited girl more touchy than to start giving her orders." He disapprovingly shook his head. "My God, Jessie, I thought you had more sense."

Jessie's cheeks really burned now. He could admit to himself that he had been all wrong, but he didn't want to sit here talking about it. "Will you drop it?" he yelped. He stood and stomped to his sheepskin coat, hanging on the rack.

"Sure you don't want to tell me a little more?" There was mockery in Asa's voice.

"All I want is a little peace," Jessie flung back as he threw open the door. Every time her name was mentioned, it drove a root of loneliness deeper into his mind. Lord, she had been a pretty thing before she went away. The absence had only improved her. Her beauty seemed to have deepened and taken on a new maturity.

He stopped and looked disbelievingly at the sky. The day was not only mild, it seemed to be softer. A breeze caressed his face, and he didn't want to shrink from it. It was hard to believe, but it looked as though spring had finally arrived.

If it had arrived, it opened the season to a lot of hard work. Not only would the ewes start lambing, but the shearing season wouldn't be far behind. He would go from dawn to dark, then stagger to bed completely exhausted. He'd better check the herders' wagons, used when the flocks were moved to summer grazing. They were small huts on wheels, for the herders wouldn't come in until the weather drove them back for the winter. If he recalled properly, some of those wagons needed repairs.

He passed Deke moving that small flock out again. The combined blatting of the sheep was raucous, but it was a pleasant sound to hear after such a long absence.

"Find enough grass yesterday to make it worthwhile, Deke?"

Deke gave him that gaping grin. "I found a hell of a patch of grass yesterday. They didn't eat it all. I figure I'm saving a lot of hay. Besides, it did them a lot of good. About this time of the year they get downright hungry for something green."

Jessie nodded. Deke had herded sheep for more years than Jessie had been alive. A good sheepherder was always conscious of the welfare of his flock.

"Thought I'd look over the huts, Deke, and see what repairs they need."

"Fix mine," Deke said sternly. "I told you last fall that damned roof was leaking."

Jessie sighed. Deke had told him, but the winter had come fast and severe, shutting off most of the outside work. Jessie wouldn't be surprised to find a long list of repairs. "I'll take care of it, Deke," he promised.

Deke moved his flock on out. His whistling carried back to Jessie. There went a happy man. His needs were simple. He didn't have a lot of material things, nor did he want them. There might be a lesson in Deke's simple life, Jessie thought soberly. He knew he wouldn't change. He didn't know what put that inner drive in him, but it demanded he keep on reaching out for more. Maybe being born a Kilmer ensured that.

There were six wagons lined up under the big shed. The Kilmers ran six flocks of sheep, and each herder had his own wagon. The wagons were wider than ordinary wagons, and the hut was built on it. Two people could crowd into it, but it was much more comfortable for a lone man. A bunk was at the far end, and a stovepipe extended through the roof from the cookstove on the floor. A table and chair and a cupboard completed the furnishings. It made for a lonely life, but a sheepherder was satisfied with it. Those kind of men didn't need company to fill out their lives. Some herders became efficient cooks, and others were extensive readers. Jessie knew he would find in some of the huts elaborate libraries. He shook his head at the thought of the span of lonely hours a sheepherder faced. But they seemingly liked it, for they hired on year after year. The pay wasn't much, but then, neither was a sheepherder's needs.

Jessie completed his inspection of this wagon. He found nothing wrong except for a couple of loose sideboards. He made a note as to its repairs. He moved on to another wagon. He muttered a grateful thanks as he found it in top shape. The wagons would have to be stocked with supplies, and just the stocking of them took considerable effort. The wagons weren't driven far daily. A sheepherder would drive to a spot where the surrounding grass was good. Then the wagon wasn't used, except for sleeping and eating quarters until the grass was cropped short. Then the wagon would be moved. The sheepherder took his flock out about six miles a day, walking every foot of the way. He would take the sheep out three miles, moving slowly to let them graze. Then he would move them back to the wagon for corralling at night. He had constructed his corral the first night after his arrival. It was a simple matter, consisting of widely spaced stakes driven into the ground, then stretching long runs of muslin to form the corral. It wasn't a stout affair, but it was enough to contain the sheep for the night. Corralling them at night gave the sheepherder the advantage of having them under his eyes. His use of a sheep dog made everything more workable. The dog's keen nose could smell any predator. He would bark furiously at any intrusion. Many times the barking chased the predators away. It also alerted the sheepherder, and he would step out of the wagon and blast away with his gun. It didn't matter whether or not he actually saw the intruder. The reports of the gun would scare the predator away. Coyotes and wolves were the worst offenders. Occasionally a bear would wander in, and he could do tremendous damage. A bear didn't scare very well. If a sheepherder couldn't get him to run, he would be sick when he surveyed the loss. There had been several occasions when a bear standing its ground had killed a sheepherder who wasn't a crack shot. If he only wounded the bear, the animal became enraged, one of the most awesome forces in the animal world.

Jessie shook his head as all those things ran through his mind. Many of the facts he had picked up through actual experience; the rest had been passed on down to him by tongue, mostly from Asa. A sheepherder's life was a hard one, and the material rewards weren't that good. But still, men clung to it, owner and sheepherder. You're clinging to it, he accused himself. He had been raised to it, and he knew nothing else to do.

Under Asa's tutelage, he had learned every plant that grew in Wyoming. There seemed to be as many poisonous weeds as there was grass. Five kinds of death camas could be found all over Wyoming. Just a nibble of that poisonous weed could kill a sheep. Fortunately, death camas grew sparsely. The lupines were on the list of deadly poisons. Sheep could eat them in early spring, but when the bean pods formed, they were deadly. Then there was arrow grass and chokecherry. Worst of all was the locoweed. There were three kinds of that—white, purple and blue. The white was the worst of them. If the grass was good, sheep would avoid the worst patches. But if sheep got into it, owners suffered loss. A good herder kept his sheep away from locoweed. Eating locoweed drove a sheep crazy, followed by death. On top of the poisonous weeds were a long list of plants that caused just as much trouble. Some of those plants had sharp spines that punctured the skin, leaving an opening for fungi.

There was squirreltail, awn grass, sticktights, cockleburs, puncture vine, and a lot of cactuses. Other woody plants balled up and caused stomach irritation. Jessie smiled sourly. The list was endless. Add pingue, mullein, soapweed to that list. Turkey mullein formed a mass of matter sheep couldn't digest. Jessie had seen twenty such balls as big as hickory nuts from the stomach of one sick sheep.

Jessie shook his head. Looking at that formidable list, it was a miracle that a man could successfully raise sheep against all those odds.

Hell, Jessie thought in irritation. It was too bad a man couldn't know about all those things before he went into the sheep-raising business. If he had known, he would never even have considered taking such risks.

He inspected Deke's wagon last and swore as he found the state the roof was in. The first spring rain would thoroughly soak the interior. That roof had to be repaired immediately.

Jessie made another penciled notation on his growing list. Damn this business. For every foot a man gained, he slipped back a couple.

After searching through all the outbuildings, his swearing was more vicious. They were out of everything. He would have to make a trip into town. Not only was that a nuisance, it would take money. He groaned as he thought of the meager amount of money in the bank.

He stamped into the kitchen, and Asa was busy stirring up a cake. He glanced at Jessie and observed, "I can see where you didn't have a very happy morning."

"You wouldn't either if you found out what I did," Jessie growled. "I just finished checking the wagons. Look at this list." He held out the piece of paper. "All repairs to make," he finished heatedly.

"Nothing new," Asa said easily. "Doesn't it happen every spring?"

"They weren't like this one," Jessie snapped. "We haven't any supplies left."

Asa's voice sharpened. "Then go into town and buy what you need."

"With what?" Jessie's voice kept rising. "I told you how little we've got in the bank."

Asa wasn't perturbed. "Then charge it. We always have before."

Jessie stalked to a chair and sat down. "I'm getting damned tired of always being short of money. Doesn't that ever bother you?"

Asa limped over to the table and sat down across from Jessie. "Of course it does. No man likes to be pinched. But things are a lot better than they used to be. You should have seen the way things were when I first came out to this country."

Jessie sighed. He had heard that story countless times, but he knew he was going to hear it again.

Asa's keen old ears caught the sound of that small sigh. He roared, "Damn it. You're like all the young ones today. You think you know it all. You can't learn anything from an old man."

Jessie looked down at the table. He wouldn't willingly hurt the old man's feelings for anything in the world. "I didn't mean it that way," he said in small apology.

Asa wasn't that easily soothed, for he still sounded testy. But he made an effort. "You sure sounded like it. How about me fixing a ham sandwich?" He thought he read signs of refusal in Jessie's face and said in argument, "It'd save you the cost of having to eat in a restaurant. That would keep you from having to worry more about spending money."

"Well, all right," Jessie said grudgingly. He watched Asa slice the ham. He swore at himself for the dissension between them. Asa did the best he could, and rarely was he grumpy. Jessie had been moody about the shape of their equipment, and he had taken out his ill-temper on the old man. No, this was all his fault.

"Good-looking ham," he remarked as Asa brought the sandwiches to the table and went back for the coffeepot.

Asa poured two cups before he sat down. "I thought so while I was baking it. Better than the last couple we had. Not as salty."

Jessie bit into his sandwich. "Never tasted better ham."

Asa tasted his sandwich. "Pretty damned good if I do say so myself."

Jessie had eaten half of his sandwich before he could get the apologetic words out. "Grandpa, I'm sorry. I was taking out my unhappiness on you. But damn it, I'd like to see some progress."

"Know exactly how you feel, son," Asa remarked.

Jessie's eyebrows rose, and his resentment returned. "How would *you* know?"

"Hah," Asa scoffed. "Don't you think I was ever young once? I kept pushing to make things happen faster."

"I know you were," Jessie replied. "But I don't think you had it as tough as it is now. Things came along then a little easier."

Asa gripped the edge of the table until his knuckles stood out whitely. His temper was mounting again. "You don't think we had it tough? Maybe you've heard this story before, but you're going to listen to it again."

Jessie couldn't help but sigh once more. He resigned himself to a boring recounting.

"Do you know how I started, Jessie? I was a common sheepherder and damned glad to get that job. You've never had to take orders, you've always been on the other end. I built up the Kilmer land from that poor start. It took years, and you think I never fretted about the lack of progress?"

Jessie doggedly set to finishing his sandwich. If he made any comment, it would only prolong the ordeal.

"I got my start from raising my first bummie. You know what a bummie is, don't you?"

"I know," Jessie said with no give in his tone. Did Asa think he had forgotten everything he learned? Bummies were the motherless lambs, orphaned for one reason or another.

"His mother just laid down and died," Asa went on. "Or a predator got her. The flock owner usually gave away the bummies he had. The owner didn't want the bother of raising it. My boss gave me the first bummie I had. I can't tell you how many hours of sleep that bummie cost me. I was up several times a night, seeing that he had enough to eat and was warm enough. I raised him. But before I did, I had five others to raise. I made my first shipment that fall. I shipped six head with the owner's shipment." He grinned wickedly at Jessie. "And you complain about the lack of progress. Don't try to tell me things were easier then."

Jessie put all his attention on drinking his coffee. "Aw, I'm sorry, Grandpa," he mumbled. "I guess I was down really low this morning." He had heard the story before, but he hadn't really paid it a lot of attention. He had had some experience with raising bummies. They required a lot of attention. He looked at Asa with new respect. My God, Asa had a lot of drive. "You didn't start out with eight thousand acres, Grandpa."

Asa snorted. "I sure didn't. Wasn't nobody around then to hand you anything. I homesteaded a hundred and sixty acres. Kept my job as a sheepherder too. Believe me, my hands were full. But I proved up on that piece. Then I set out with an ambition in mind. I didn't want all the land in the world. Just the land that adjoined mine." He grinned in delight at remembering the old days. "That boundary kept growing bigger. Then one of those mornings I woke up and decided I'd acquired enough land."

"You never sold any of it, Grandpa?"

"Hell, you couldn't have pried a foot of it out of my hands. Though during the war with the cattlemen, I had some big doubts. For a while, it looked like I was going to lose all of it. I had one purpose in mind that made me hang on."

"What purpose was that?"

"One of these days, all this land is going to belong to you," Asa said solemnly. "Don't look so startled. Haven't you ever thought of that?"

Jessie swallowed hard. "If I did, it wasn't very seriously. I guess I figured on you living forever, Grandpa."

"You know better than that," Asa said fiercely. "If you want to really know how I feel, get married and raise a son. Then you'll know why I clung to this land."

Jessie swallowed hard. There was another new thought. "Maybe that'll happen someday," he said slowly. "What was your biggest thrill, Grandpa?"

Asa ruminated over that a moment. "I guess it was when I first got my Ohio Merion rams. I scraped the bottom of the barrel to get enough to send off for them. Never regretted a penny of it. Those rams doubled my wool production and almost doubled the weight of my marketable lambs." He thought he saw a question forming in Jessie's eyes. "Hell, yes, it was worth it. I'd do it all over the same way. I know what's grinding you. A livestock grower never has any money until he markets his crop. Then he only holds it long enough to pay off his bills. Oh, he can see a big wad of money when he sells out. But very few growers see that. They leave everything they have to a relative." Asa shook his head in reflection. "No, he spends all his life in seeing that his holdings grow bigger and bigger. That's his satisfaction, or in improving his stock. You'll never get out of it, Jessie. You were born to sheep raising, and you'll die doing the same thing."

Jessie wanted to say Asa was wrong in thinking that, but he couldn't argue with the old man, not after listening to him as long as he had.

"Another sandwich?" Asa asked.

Jessie shook his head and stood. "I'd better be getting started if I want to get back by night. I'm taking the light wagon."

"Take whatever you need. And quit stewing over things. One of these days the sun will break out, and you'll wonder whatever possessed you to mope around."

Jessie grinned twistedly. "I hope you're right." He went out and closed the door behind him.

He thought about Asa's words all the way to town. Asa could be right in everything he said. Maybe the best goal a man could erect would be in doing for somebody else. But he couldn't see how that could ever happen to him. Once he had begun to think seriously about Beth. But her leaving had broken that up; that and the argument over Grat Hagen. It had been a shock to see her again. She had grown so beautiful that he was awed. No, nothing would ever happen there. He would keep his mind locked against the possibility.

He drove up to Roark Summers' lumber yard, jumped down and tied the team to a hitch rack. Summers was doing a thriving business, growing bigger every year. Jessie's eyes widened in amazement. He'd be damned if Summers hadn't added to his building during the winter.

He walked inside the crowded room, and Summers was busy arranging merchandise on a shelf. He saw Jessie, dropped what he was doing, and hurried up to him.

"Jessie," he said in greeting and extended a hand. "Been quite a while since you've been in." He was a big man with a genial manner. Very few people disliked him.

"The winter kept me tied down pretty good," Jessie said, wringing the proffered hand.

"It was a hell of a one, wasn't it?" Summers said. "What can I do for you?"

"I need quite a few supplies, Roark. Lumber, tarpaper, nails."

"You just name what you want."

"You haven't heard all of it yet, Roark. I'm going to have to charge it. Probably won't be able to pay for it until after the first shipment of lambs."

Summers made a deprecatory sweep of his hand. "Most of the county is on my books. You won't be any different than anybody else."

"Don't you ever worry about those bills never being met?" Jessie asked curiously.

"I learned a long time ago that I couldn't remember what I worried about a year ago. It's useless to worry about things that don't stick with you any longer than that."

"It's a good outlook," Jessie said soberly. "Maybe I ought to try it. I did a fool thing the other day. It cost me good."

"That fight with Grat?" Summers asked. "I heard all about that. You fined for that fight?"

"Both of us were." The memory refreshed Jessie's anger. "Those damned Hagens. The judge warned me never to get into another fight with them. If I never see a Hagen again, it'll suit me just fine."

He went about the store with Summers, ordering the items he wanted. He kept wincing as another item was added to his bill.

He came to the bottom of the list and said, "I guess that about does it, Roark."

He groaned hollowly as Summers added up the purchases and announced the total. How in the hell could a man stop worrying with such figures hovering about him, ready to pounce on him at the first slip?

Summers helped Jessie carry his purchases out to the wagon. Only a few more items were left inside, and Jessie said sourly, "I can handle them." He signed for the purchases and said glumly, "Looks like I tried to buy out the store."

"You don't hear me complaining," Summers said cheerfully.

"Sure," Jessie said, picked up the last few items, and walked out of the store. He wouldn't be complaining either if he stood in Summers' shoes.

He stowed the last few articles in the wagon, turned, and Beth was watching him.

"Hello," he said stiffly.

Her eyes darkened. "You haven't forgiven me for going after Raines, have you, Jessie?"

"Should I?" His voice grew colder.

"I had to, Jessie," she said earnestly. "It was an awful fight. I was afraid one of you would be seriously hurt."

He stared at her, unforgiving. "Was it fear that something would happen to Grat?"

Her anger made her face flame. "The same old stupid complaint."

"You called me that once before," he said ungraciously.

"I did not," she denied.

"Oh yes, you did. Just before you went away to school you said you didn't want to wind up as stupid as some of the people in this county."

She got her temper under control, for she said helplessly, "I wasn't referring to you, Jessie. You should know that."

He smiled bleakly at her. "How could I? I'm one of the dumb ones."

"Oh, you're hopeless," she said, a spark coming back into her voice. She whirled and was almost running as she went down the street.

Jessie watched her until she was out of sight. That ended all possibility of anything ever happening between them. If he ever raised a family, it wouldn't be with her.

He climbed into the wagon and backed it out. How could anything ever happen between them when they couldn't get beyond the first unhappy words?

He snapped the reins on the team's rumps. "Oh, to hell with it all," he said savagely.

CHAPTER 10

Curt hummed contentedly as he moved down the street. He had completed all his shopping, and that included buying three saddle horses and a packhorse. The buying of the food supplies plus the livestock had put a huge dent in his little hoard. He knew damned well he was going to speak to Jacob about this.

He didn't know Jacob was anywhere near until a voice said from behind him, "It's taking you long enough to get about the job you agreed to."

Curt knew that voice too well to be startled. He turned and said easily, "Hello, Jacob. I was hoping to see you again."

"You shouldn't want to see me now," Keeley growled. "I thought you made a deal. It's been four days since I gave you that money. Money you haven't done a damned thing to earn."

Curt's face hardened. Jacob had changed so much since the days he knew him that it was hard to keep his temper under control. "You jump to conclusions pretty quick, don't you, Jacob?"

Keeley flushed. "As far as I can see, you haven't done anything but hang around town. I warned you, Curt." His voice rose shrilly until with each word he was panting.

Curt wanted to reach out and shake some sense into his head. "You think I could just go out and start the moment you gave me the go-ahead? I had to wait until Young and Royal got here. That took a couple of days. Then I had to buy weapons, camping equipment, horses and food. I've spent over six hundred dollars for those items."

Keeley could feel his throat constricting. "What do you expect me to do, pay that extra money?"

"Exactly," Curt said, unperturbed. "You didn't tell me anything about those extra expenses. I don't think I should have to pay for them."

Keeley obstinately shook his head. "I gave you ample money to cover all that." He looked around hastily. The street was still empty.

He could go on talking to Curt. "I won't do it," he said heatedly.

"Fine," Curt said easily. "Then I won't do the job you proposed."

Keeley could feel a stabbing pain in the vicinity of his heart, and his breathing was becoming more difficult. "All I have to do is to tell the local law about you," he threatened.

His eyes widened in amazement. Curt's eyes were filled with laughter. "Aren't you forgetting something, little brother? I can do some talking myself. I'll tell the sheriff about the job you want me to do."

It felt as though a great hand was inexorably closing about Keeley's throat. "You wouldn't do that," he said weakly.

Curt's eyes darkened. "What about the money I spent?"

Keeley's eyes darted frantically to the end of the block. Somebody had just turned onto this street. He couldn't stay here any longer talking to Curt. "You'll get it," he said huskily. "Just go ahead and do what I asked."

The gleam in Curt's eyes grew brighter. At last he had found a way to handle Jacob; just keep a threat dangling over his head. "We're leaving in the morning, Jacob. But I'll get in touch with you. About my money—"

Keeley broke into a rapid walk. "Can't talk here any longer," he muttered. He brushed by Curt, and Curt slowly turned to watch him go. Ah, he thought as he saw the oncoming pedestrian. Little brother can't afford to be seen with me. It was another little item to file in his mind.

He nodded pleasantly to the pedestrian as he reached him. "Wonderful day, isn't it, sir?"

"It is that," the man replied. "Didn't I see you talking to Jacob Keeley?"

Jacob had disappeared. "That wasn't Keeley," Curt said.

"I'll swear it was him," the pedestrian muttered. "Maybe my eyes are failing."

"I hope not," Curt replied gravely. He nodded to the man and went on his way. Merriment rose inside him until he wanted to laugh aloud. He had found a way to handle his dear little brother. Jacob's treatment of him had been an irritating thing. Maybe he would try to see Jacob before he left town. But that could be postponed. He wanted to look over the Kilmer place and see what faced him. He would see Jacob again. He made a mental promise. From here on, he ceased being subservient to Jacob. He was back where he belonged; he had reestablished authority over Jacob.

Young wasn't the horseman that Royal was, but he had enough basic skill to get him where Curt wanted him to go. Royal slouched easily in the saddle, looking over the rest of the stock with open disfavor. "I can say one thing," he said caustically. "We're still going first-class."

Curt kept his annoyance from putting a bite in his tone. "They'll do what we want. They'll take us there and bring us back," he finished in a clipped voice.

Royal saw that maybe he had pushed Curt too far. "Sure, they will," he agreed easily. "How far do we ride?"

"As I got it, about fifteen miles due east. We're looking for a sheep ranch. The house and outbuildings aren't too much."

"Do we ride up and ask, Who lives here?" Royal asked.

"We do not," Curt said sharply. "We want to keep out of sight all we can. If we're never seen at all, it'll be that much better for us."

Young uttered a distressed bleat.

"Come on," Curt said, annoyed. "You knew what you were getting into from the start."

"Young scares easy," Royal said sardonically.

Young's face flamed. "You keep your mouth off me," he said shrilly. "Maybe it's too bad you don't show as much sense as I do."

Royal's face turned ugly, and Curt stepped in. "Stop that damned bickering. Maybe we don't like each other, but we're going to work together. After the job's done, you can claw each other to pieces. I don't give a damn."

That restored Royal's humor, for he grinned. "I'm sorry I walked on your toes, Young."

"All right," Young said sullenly. "I just wanted you to know that I won't stand for much more of that."

Royal's face twisted in sudden anger, and Curt stopped a further outbreak by saying, "I said, That was enough of that."

Both of them fell silent. Oh, damn it, Curt thought. It wasn't going to be a pleasant time. These two would be constantly at each other's throat. He rode in silent reflection. Prison had changed both of them. They hadn't quarreled so freqently before prison. Adversity brought out the weakness in a man's nature. Maybe it's changed you too, he thought. He could grant that, but he tried to keep a close guard on emotions that could too easily surface. Maybe it would be a spur to get this over as quickly as possible.

They rode the remaining distance in silence, breaking it only occasionally with a grunt. Maybe the silence was better than picking at each other.

"Sure you haven't missed it?" Royal asked. "Seems to me we've come a hell of a way."

Curt frowned at him. All their tempers were on a hair-fine trigger. Maybe action would keep them occupied.

"We haven't seen any outfits, have we?" he asked. "We'll see what we want any minute now. Hah," he said in small triumph. "That has to be it up ahead."

The fringe of trees had thickened, but through them he had caught a glimpse of a house and outbuildings. Jacob had been right when he said the Kilmers ran a sorry outfit.

He picked his way to the edge of the fringe, careful not to step out into the open where somebody might catch a glimpse of him. The other two came up behind him, and he shook his head as a warning, pointing at the buildings, then placed a forefinger across his lips.

They immediately caught his meaning, for neither of them spoke. The three remained motionless for quite a period, studying the buildings. They saw several people move about the buildings, and a herder started a flock of sheep away from the house. Even at this distance, the blatting of the sheep carried faintly to them.

Curt gingerly turned his horse and at a slow walk moved farther back into the woods.

"Is that the outfit you wanted?" Royal asked. At Curt's nod, he added, "Don't look like much."

"They run a lot of sheep," Curt grunted. "You saw some of them being driven out."

"What do we do now?" Royal asked.

"I guess start earning our money," Curt answered. "We'd better see where that flock is going."

They had the direction the sheep were driven in, and before long they cut the tracks of tiny hoofs.

"Don't see where there's enough grass to make it worthwhile driving them out for," Royal commented.

"I guess the herder knows where he's going," Curt replied absently. He didn't have anything definite in mind. Even after they picked up the sheep again, he hadn't the slightest idea of what he would do.

The blatting grew stronger, carrying back distinctly to them. They had slowed their pace to a slow walk, constantly fighting the horses to keep them dragged down to this pace.

Royal suddenly stood in the stirrups and stabbed a finger ahead. Curt nodded. He had already picked up the dirty white of the flock just a short distance ahead. Royal looked questioningly at him, and Curt shook his head. He didn't know what he was going to do.

They followed the sheep to a small valley, hemmed in by three steep cliffs. On the far side, there was a precipitous drop. From here, Curt couldn't tell how steep that drop was, but his pulses quickened. Nature was shaping a plan in his head. Just a short drop should be enough to accomplish what he wanted done.

He pulled back until he was certain the horsemen wouldn't be seen and conversed in a low tone.

"Did you see that drop at one side of that little valley?" he asked.

Royal nodded. "Looks like a pretty steep one. You planning on driving the sheep over it?"

Curt grinned wickedly. Royal caught on quick. "How many sheep do you think is in that bunch?"

Royal scowled. "I'd say at least a couple of hundred."

Curt nodded. "After we get them on a dead run they ought to sail into that drop."

"That won't cause much damage," Royal objected.

"It's a start, isn't it?" Curt said flatly.

Young was fidgeting over something that was on his mind. "Suppose somebody sees us?"

Royal grinned savagely. "There he goes again."

"Nobody will see us," Curt said practically. "Did you see anybody on the way here? This is pretty lonesome country. We'll wait until the sheep settle a little."

They waited a half hour, then edged closer. The sheep had bunched up, feeding close to the edge of the precipice.

"Do you see the herder?" Curt asked. He had been scanning the little valley pretty closely and hadn't picked him up yet.

"There he is," Royal said suddenly.

Curt saw the figure blending with the brush. "Keep an eye on him. When we burst down into the valley, he's liable to object. And he's probably got a gun."

He heard the bleat of distress Young made. This time Royal ignored the sound of worry. "How do we handle him?" he demanded.

"We'll run him over the drop with the sheep," Curt answered harshly.

That didn't completely satisfy Royal. "What if he tries to protect them? I thought I saw a rifle in his hands."

"Then we shoot him," Curt replied savagely. He sucked in a deep breath. "Let's go."

They came down the slope at a headlong gallop, all three yelling at the top of their lungs. Curt saw the figure stiffen and take a couple of steps. Curt saw him raise a rifle to his shoulder. The man didn't fully complete the action for Royal stood in the stirrups and loosed three quick shots. The distance wasn't too far, and he didn't miss at that range.

Curt didn't know which shot got the herder, but he crumpled to the ground. Royal yelled in some kind of primitive pleasure.

At the sound of the horses' hoofs, the sheep had stopped their grazing, raising their heads. It took only an instant for terror to grip them. They whirled and broke into a run, the three horsemen closely pursuing them. The horsemen cut off any attempt to break back, and they pushed them relentlessly toward the drop. The sheep came closer and closer to the edge. The first of them dropped out of sight, and the oncoming horses pushed the others in the same direction. The terrorized bleating of the sheep filled the air, and the last of them fell out of sight.

Curt pulled his horse to a stop at the edge. He was breathing hard. That was the start of his job. Jacob should be well pleased.

He dismounted and looked over the drop. It was farther down than he imagined. The drop had killed most of the sheep. For a moment he couldn't see any movement in that dirty gray mass. Then, here and there, a few individual animals struggled to regain their feet. Most of them didn't make it. If they did regain their feet, it was only momentary, for they fell back. Curt suspected broken bones were the cause, and a few did manage to get to their feet, then slowly walked away. Curt doubted there was a half-dozen survivors.

Royal threw his rifle to his shoulder, and Curt stopped him. "What do you think you're doing?"

"Some of them are getting away. I thought I'd drop them."

That made Curt inordinately angry. "Let them go. A few head won't make that much difference."

Royal lowered his rifle. "Well, if you want to turn in a sloppy job."

"Let *me* judge that," Curt snapped. "I want to see about that herder."

They walked over to where the herder lay. He lay on his stomach, his face pressed against the ground. Royal turned him over, and the front of his shirt was a solid red. "Got him dead center," Royal bragged. "Pretty good shooting, if I do say so. That was on the run."

"That's going to cost us," Young said shrilly. "When they find him, they'll be looking for us. You know what they'll do to us."

"Suppose you tell me," Royal sneered.

They were on the verge of another entanglement, and Curt stepped between them.

"I'd go along with us, Young," Curt said levelly. "Without any fuss. You'll be considered in this as much as we are."

Young wilted visibly. "I didn't want to go in on this from the start," he moaned.

"You're in it now," Curt said. He turned to Royal and said, "I'll give you a hand with the body."

"What are you going to do with him?" Royal asked.

"Make it a little more difficult for them to find him. I want to throw him after the sheep."

Royal brightened. "A sound thought," he approved. He took the herder's feet, and Curt grabbed the arms. The man was surprisingly light.

They swung him back and forth twice, then Curt barked, "Now."

They simultaneously loosened their grip and the body sailed out into space.

Curt looked down at the dead sheep. He could barely pick out the herder's body. That would make it more difficult to find the man.

Young moaned again, and Curt turned savagely on him. "You can stick with us, Young, or you can go it alone. Remember this! A lone man will be a lot easier to pick up."

Young's mouth hung open, and he started to say something. "One more thing," Curt said in a cold voice. "We don't want to hear any more of your complaining from now on. Now, we'd better get out of here. We'll lay low until we hear the results of how this turned out."

They mounted and turned the horses uphill. Young had heard everything Curt told him, but he kept looking back. Curt's palms were sweating. He had to untie the packhorse and get out of there. Curt wanted to make tonight's camp as far off of Kilmer's land as he could.

CHAPTER 11

Jessie walked to the window and peered out at the sky. This was the half-dozenth trip he had made.

"Something bothering you?" Asa asked.

Jessie started to deny the charge, then reconsidered. Asa had every right to know what was going on.

"Deke's not back in," he said, his voice tight. "It's less than an hour till sundown."

Asa didn't worry as readily as Jessie. "Deke never hurries. He'll be ambling in any minute now."

Jessie refused to believe that. Deke was as reliable as a good clock. Something had happened to detain him like this.

Asa frowned at the determination in Jessie's face. "Nothing I can say will change your mind. I knew all along you were going after him. Of all the stubborn—" He broke off at Jessie's grin. "What are you grinning about?"

"It tickles me to hear you blame me for that stubbornness. Got a right to it. I inherited it. I got it from Pa, and you handed it down to him." He broke into delighted laughter at Asa's swearing.

"Swear all you want, but you can't deny it. Asa, if you were looking for Deke, where would you start? He told me he'd found a patch of early grass and was taking advantage of it."

Asa's forehead furrowed as he thought. "My guess would be that little valley surrounded by three hills. The other side drops off pretty abruptly. As protected as that valley is, it could mean early grass."

Jessie nodded. From Asa's description, he knew exactly where that valley was.

He walked over and took his sheepskin off the rack. With the sun going down, it could get chilly in a hurry.

"You take someone with you," Asa ordered. The set of his face said that he was beginning to worry now.

Jessie jammed his hat on his head. "I will," he said in a grim voice.

He found Miller and Mendoza at the herders' bunkhouse and explained briefly what was bothering him. "Deke's not in yet," he said tersely. "It's not like Deke to try and wring the last minute out of the day."

Both men nodded soberly. They were herders, and from experience they knew any one of a hundred things could have happened to delay Deke—all of them bad.

"Do you know which direction he took?" Miller asked. He was a stringbean of a man, with a face set in moody lines. He preferred to be alone. He had chosen the right business.

"Deke found an early patch of grass," Jessie said.

"That'd have to be hidden valley," both men said simultaneously. "It has grass first of anyplace I know of," Mendoza finished. He had a soft voice and soft eyes, but he was as good as any man Jessie knew, tough and reliable in an emergency.

"Let's get saddled up," Jessie said. "We haven't much light left." He didn't have to tell them to bring their rifles. Both men grabbed for them as automatically as they reached for their hats.

The last light of the day wasn't an enduring one, particularly at this time of the year. Once the sun started sinking, it seemed to accelerate its descent. Jessie could swear the darkness had crept up appreciably on them.

They saddled, and Jessie headed for the small valley, not trying to save the horses. All the way there, he kept praying he'd see Deke and his flock coming toward them. The relief would be so great that Jessie wouldn't even bawl him out.

The light was almost gone when Jessie pulled up on the bluff, overlooking the valley. As much as he strained his eyes he couldn't see a thing, at least not the thing he was looking for. Questioning looks at Miller and Mendoza brought him nothing but negative shakes of their heads.

"Let's go down," he said, touching his horse with his spurs. The animal went gingerly down the slope, digging in its hoofs. Jessie leaned far back to help the horse retain his footing. He didn't blame the animal's reluctance. This slope was steep, and the bad light hampered his sight.

He made it safely down, and Miller and Mendoza joined him. Jessie stood in the stirrups and yelled, "Deke, Deke." His voice slammed from the slopes surrounding the valley to resound mockingly. Miller and Mendoza added their voices, and the echoes hammered at a man's ears.

"Spread out," Jessie ordered. "Keep yelling."

The darkness was complete when they finally met again. "Nothing?" Jessie asked. He got no response from them, but the sense of defeat was powerful enough to send out negative waves of its own.

"I passed the edge of the drop," Jessie muttered. "I didn't dare get too close in the darkness."

"I was by that way too," Mendoza said softly.

Jessie frowned as he remembered the eerie feeling as he had paused above the empty space over the drop. He had felt a strange pull, but he hadn't been able to see anything.

"Shall we look again?" Miller asked.

Jessie shook his head. "It wouldn't do any good. If Deke was anywhere near, he would've heard us."

"Do you think he went someplace else?" Miller asked.

Jessie's fears had increased, and they goaded him into insensitive anger. "How would I know?" he yelled. "I'm sorry, Carl," he said immediately. "This is driving me crazy."

Miller nodded, his face perturbed. "I know. What do we do now?"

"Go back home. There's nothing else we can do. We'll start again in the morning."

It was a silent ride home, each man busy with his thoughts. "I'll unsaddle him, Jessie," Miller offered.

It was proof of Miller's forgiveness. "Thanks, Carl. I'd like to get in. I imagine Asa is eaten up wondering what became of us."

He opened the kitchen door and Asa's back was toward him. He heard Jessie's entrance and he turned instantly. "Bad, huh?" he grunted after seeing Jessie's face.

"Does it show that much, Asa?"

"I could scrape it off with a stick. Did you get to the valley?"

"We were over it three different times. Yelled our lungs out. No answer of any kind. I'm going back there in the morning."

Asa's eyes narrowed. "A particular reason?"

Jessie raised and dropped his hands helplessly. "I don't know. I stood at the edge of that drop. I couldn't see into it. The darkness came too fast, but I had the strangest feeling of something down there pulling at me." He glanced at Asa, half expecting him to ridicule him for such a crazy idea.

"Then I'd go back," Asa said promptly. "It's called intuition in a woman. I don't know what it's called in a man. Maybe a hunch. I know I've ignored that feeling a couple of times and I regretted it. I'll get your supper ready."

"I'm not hungry," Jessie replied listlessly.

"You gotta eat," Asa stormed. "You gotta keep your strength up. You don't know what you'll need tomorrow."

Asa was right, and Jessie gave in. "Not too much," he cautioned. "Something light and fast."

"How about some eggs and bacon? I can have that ready in a hurry."

Maybe it was the aroma of the frying bacon, but Jessie felt his belly rumble. Asa set a plate before him and ordered, "Fall to."

Each bite increased the reach of Jessie's appetite, and he ate voraciously. He finished and said half-ashamedly, "I'm glad you didn't listen to me."

"Feel better?" At Jessie's nod, Asa said, "I don't know what it is, but there's some direct connection between a man's mind and his belly. If the belly feels better, the mind thinks it does too."

Jessie grinned and asked, "When do you think I'll get old enough to quit arguing with you?"

Asa chuckled. "Probably never. You better turn in. You want to be up early in the morning."

"Can't argue with that," Jessie said and rose to his feet.

Jessie spent most of the night seeking sleep. He'd roll to a new position, punch his pillow, and fight some more sleepless time. He couldn't stop the worry that so viciously fought the onslaught of slumber. Where was Deke? Had something bad happened to his flock? He swore at himself for the futility of this. He wouldn't know anything at all until daylight came.

He dozed off a little before dawn, and was hollow-eyed when he finally arose. He dressed and walked into the kitchen. Asa took one look at him. "Been fighting it all night, haven't you?"

"Something like that," Jessie admitted.

"Sit down. I'll have the first batch of flapjacks ready in a minute."

The kitchen was filled with the good smells of frying ham. Asa put a big stack of griddle cakes on Jessie's plate and placed a thick slice of ham beside them. "You eat," Asa commanded. "We're not going through that again this morning."

He kept the flapjacks coming until Jessie threw up a hand. "No more," he begged. "I can't handle them."

"You did pretty fair," Asa conceded. "That oughta hold you for a good spell."

Jessie nodded. "Have Miller and Mendoza shown up yet?"

"They ate a good spell ago. They're probably waiting outside for you."

Damn that restless night. It had cost him an earlier start. It made him look pretty slothful before his help. He walked outside, and Miller and Mendoza had his horse saddled.

"How'd you sleep?" Jessie asked as they started out.

"Good," Miller responded.

"Not bad," Mendoza answered.

The response made Jessie tight-lipped. Of the three, he was the only one showing laxness. Oh, he could justify himself. He was one of the owners of the flock. Deke's welfare was his responsibility. That poor night of sleeping was one of the costs of ownership.

They didn't speak again until they reached the valley.

"Do you want to spread out?" Miller asked.

Jessie shook his head. "I want to see what's down that drop first."

That eerie feeling, a dread of seeing what could be lying down there, returned.

All three dismounted and advanced cautiously. Jessie was the first to reach the edge. He looked down and a brutal hand squeezed his throat. By morning's light, he could plainly see what was down there. For an instant he wanted to reject the sight, but the actuality couldn't be denied. The dirty gray bodies were piled everywhere. He couldn't get a count, but he would say almost with certainty that Deke's whole flock lay down there.

Mendoza gripped his arm. "Over there, Jessie," he said, pain in his voice.

Jessie saw Deke then. He lay near the fringe of animal bodies, and there was no movement in him. What hurt Jessie the most was the fact that Deke had been there last night. It wouldn't have changed things any, a practical voice told him.

"We've got to get down there," he said in a hoarse voice.

He received two nods, and they picked their way down the slope, testing every foothold before they moved. Agonized thoughts kept pounding at Jessie's mind. What had caused this terrible accident? Deke was a good herder. He didn't have a reckless bone in his body. He would have kept the sheep away from the edge. Besides, he had the animals' instincts to help him. The sheep wouldn't have ventured too close to the edge. But all of them were down there. Something had happened to stampede the sheep over the cliff. Once blind terror had seized them, nothing could have stopped them. What had caused that blind stampede? An ugly suspicion was beginning to nibble at his thoughts. He would make no charge until he weighed his facts.

They reached the bottom and picked their way through the poor, battered bodies of the sheep. Maybe a half dozen stirred or cried pitifully. Miller and Mendoza put questioning looks on him, and Jessie knew what those unspoken words asked. What did he want done with the injured animals?

For a moment Jessie thought he would give way to unreasonable anger, he wanted to rant and rave. A man worked so damned hard to give his livestock the best treatment he could, and they wound up like this. It was difficult to get the words out of his tightly clamped lips. "Shoot them," he said flatly.

Miller and Mendoza nodded their agreement. It was the only thing that could be done. Even if the sheep could be lifted back up to the valley and carried home, it was doubtful they could be saved. It was surprising they had lived this long.

Jessie made his way to where Deke lay. Behind him he heard five shots, then after a pause, three more. There was no need for him to look to learn what was happening.

Deke lay on his stomach, his arms outflung, his neck at a queer angle. "What the hell happened, Deke?" Jessie muttered. "Did you get too close to the edge?"

He stooped and seized Deke's shoulder, then turned him over. There was a gentle reverence in his manner. His eyes widened at the massive bloodstain, and his nostrils pinched together in the rush of his breathing. Here was the answer to all of his questions. No carelessness or recklessness had killed Deke. This was an evil deed of another man.

He had to get the seething anger out of his system, and he swore at the top of his lungs, using every word at his command. Miller and Mendoza heard him swearing and came over on the run.

"What the hell—" Miller started, then his eyes dropped to the massive bloodstain on Deke's shirt. He was white-cheeked and his lips were a thin, bloodless line. "Oh, the bastard. Who do you think gunned him down, Jessie?"

It wouldn't be too hard to put a name to Miller's question. It could be only one person, or persons. "The goddamned Hagens," Jessie burst out.

Mendoza and Miller knew of Jessie's fight with Grat Hagen. They nodded solemnly. The name "Hagen" fit too well.

Jessie burned out, and his swearing stopped. "We've got to get him back up to the top." He glanced up the slope. That was going to be a brutal climb carrying the inanimate weight of a dead man.

Jessie hoped he wouldn't remember that climb. He didn't know how long it took, but the sun had climbed higher when the job was finally done. It had been a torturous climb, fighting for every secure foothold. Every now and then, Miller and Mendoza spelled each other. Jessie refused to be spelled. Deke worked for him. This was the last thing he could do for him.

"Put him on my horse behind the saddle," Jessie ordered. "I want to take him to the house."

He had trouble getting the horse to hold steady, for even though the blood was old, the smell of it made the horse go crazy. He kept dancing at the end of the reins Mendoza held, and each time Jessie and Miller tried to place Deke across the horse's rump he moved, and Deke fell to the ground.

Jessie was livid with rage. They had enough dumped on them without adding this further indignity. He cursed the horse with a passion that should have skinned him.

He ran out of breath, and reason filtered back to him. "That's not going to do any good," he said. "Sanchez, help Miller. I'll hold the bastard." He moved to the front of the horse and grabbed it by the ears. Jessie knew it hurt, and he didn't need the animal's squeal of pain to tell him so. But it worked, and he managed to hold the horse steady.

"Put Deke across the saddle," he called. "I'll ride behind Deke."

Miller and Mendoza got Deke across the saddle. Mendoza had some rope, and he cut a couple of short lengths from it. He tied Deke's dangling hands and feet together. He finished and said, "I believe that will hold him on."

He backed away, and Jessie let go of the ears. Perhaps the pain easing had its soothing effect, or the horse had determined that inanimate weight wasn't going to hurt him. He squatted, and a trembling ran through his hide in little ripples. But he no longer tried to shy or dance away.

Even as early as the day was, Jessie was dripping sweat. God, he was worn out. He vaulted up behind Deke, and Mendoza handed him the reins.

It wasn't a comfortable ride, but Jessie made it. He jumped down and tied his horse to a tie rack, then set about untying Deke. He had barely lowered the body to the ground when Asa came limping out of the house.

He looked at Deke, then faced Jessie, his eyes blazing. "Who do you think did it?"

"You put a name to the bastard."

Asa's face was so red he looked as though he would explode. "The Hagens?"

Jessie nodded. "As sure a bet as I ever saw. The whole flock was gone, driven over that drop." He waited until Miller and Mendoza approached him and said, "Take care of Deke, will you?"

"What are you going to do?" Asa asked.

"I've got to get in and talk to Quint."

"Do you think it will do any good?" Asa sounded skeptical.

"He straightened it out before," Jessie answered shortly. "It'll be better than me going after them."

"I guess you're right, son. Good luck." Asa's face was deeply troubled. Jessie nodded, then mounted. Raines was going to listen to him. By God, he was going to make him.

He raised a hand in a wave toward Asa and the other two. Damn it, would things ever settle down to normal? He didn't want to see all this trouble dumped on Asa's tired shoulders. Jessie put his horse into a fast lope. He was going to fret until he reached town and walked into Raines's office.

He stormed into Raines's office, the noise of his entrance jerking Raines's head from some paperwork. Raines surveyed Jessie calmly and drawled, "You look like you been chewing nails and are ready to spit out sparks."

"You've hit it about right," Jessie said heatedly. "I just had a herder killed and about two hundred sheep wiped out."

That hit Raines. It showed in the way he gripped the edge of his desk. "Take it easy," he begged. "When and where did this happen?"

"Sometime yesterday on our place. Some bastard, or several of them, bushwhacked Deke and stamped the flock over a sharp drop. I didn't find them until this morning. I was out to that little valley until dark. I couldn't see into the drop. When I went back this morning, there they were, Deke and the sheep."

"You say bushwhacked?" Raines asked. Oh God, it was breaking out all over again. It seemed as though it was impossible to ever get all the cussedness out of human nature.

"You got an idea of who did it, Jessie?"

Jessie hit the desk with the heel of his palm. "You're damned right I have. It was the Hagens. We found tracks of three horses. Whoever rode them shot Deke and ran the sheep over."

Raines briefly closed his eyes. He was getting tired, and he had the right to expect a little peace in his declining years. Maybe he was lucky at that. Jessie could have tore out after the Hagens instead of coming here.

"Did you or any of your men see the Hagens, Jessie?"

Jessie swallowed hard. "We didn't. As I told you, we didn't find him last night."

"Then how come you're accusing the Hagens?"

"Who else would do it?" Jessie argued. "Grat was sore ever since the trial. This was a good chance for him to get even with me."

Raines held up a hand. "Just a cockeyed minute. You haven't got any proof. All you've got is guesses."

Jessie stared incredulously at the sheriff. "This means you're not going to do anything about Deke's killing?"

"I didn't say that," Raines corrected. "I'm riding back with you. I want a look at Deke's body. Then I'll go on over to the Hagens'. If I find a shred of evidence, the Hagens will be damned sorry."

Jessie wasn't entirely appeased, but right now this was the best he could do. He would say one thing about Raines. He was a fair man. If he found anything against the Hagens, they'd pay. "Let's get started," Jessie snapped.

Raines rose from his desk and set his hat on his head. "Right with you."

CHAPTER 12

For a long moment Raines didn't say anything after he saw Deke. The flesh seemed to melt away from his face, leaving the cheekbones standing out starkly. His lips were clamped together in a tight, thin line, and his eyes were somber and brooding.

Jessie broke the silence by saying, "Do you think I'm still crazy? Wasn't he shot?"

Raines sighed. "He was shot all right."

"Do you think I'm still crazy when I think the Hagens were behind this?"

"That's still only a guess," Raines said. "I'll ride over and talk to them."

"I'll go with you," Jessie offered.

Raines shook his head.

"Why not?" Jessie demanded. "Seeing me will shake them up so much they'll admit something."

"Or warn them to be on their guard," Raines countered. "No, you stay here. I'll be back."

"I think he's trying to protect the Hagens," Jessie said furiously after Raines left.

"You don't know that," Asa pointed out. "Don't go spouting off things you can't prove. Did you ever know Raines to be unfair?"

Jessie reluctantly shook his head. "But it's damned funny he didn't want me along."

"He gave you his reasons," Asa replied. "They made sense to me." He looked at Jessie's unhappy face. "I know how you feel, son. But leave this up to Raines. He's had a lot of experience in handling just this sort of thing."

Raines stopped outside the Hagen house and looked it over. The Hagens were doing all right. The house had been freshly painted, and Raines could see nothing that needed repair.

He pounded on the back door.

Grat Hagen let him in. The Hagens must be breakfasting late this morning, for Wirt Hagen and his youngest son, Gary, were still at the table. The Chinese cook had just replenished the pancakes on their plates.

There was no real greeting in Grat's eyes. They were narrowed and mean. "To what do we owe the pleasure of this visit, Sheriff?" he asked sarcastically.

"Just happened to be passing by," Raines replied. "Thought I'd stop by and see what's going on."

Grat's snort was as eloquent as a slap in the face. "Why don't you stop putting out that stuff?" he asked derisively. "You never paid a friendly visit here in your life. Now, suppose you quit horsing around and tell us why you came."

"I came for information," Raines said levelly. "Where were you from about noon until, say, midnight yesterday?"

Wirt was a chunky man with the same blockiness of the Hagen clan. "You ain't got no right to ask us questions like that."

Raines leaned forward, his face stubborn. "I've got every right," he asserted. "If you don't want to answer, I'll find out some way."

"Hold it, Pa," Grat said. His eyes flicked to Raines. "During that time we were over at the Andersons'. It was their thirtieth anniversary. We arrived there about noon and didn't leave until after midnight. That's why we're eating so late this morning." His defiant eyes never wavered from Raines's face.

"I can check that out," Raines said easily.

Wirt slammed the table with his fists, making the dishes bounce. "Check and be damned. Did you ever know a Hagen to be a liar?"

Raines shook his head. He hadn't. But just the same he had to check out on their whereabouts. He turned to leave, and Grat asked, "You going to the Andersons'?"

"I am."

"I'm going with you," Grat said belligerently. "I want to hear everything you say."

Raines grinned bleakly. "Suit yourself."

He walked outside and waited while Grat saddled a horse. He ran the events of the last few minutes through his mind. Was Grat's reaction the mark of a guilty man, or hadn't Grat reacted naturally? Raines sighed. Right now, he didn't know.

Grat joined him and said, "This way."

"I know where the Andersons live," Raines replied testily.

They'd ridden a full mile before Grat spoke up. "Suppose you tell me what this is all about."

"You'll find out," Raines answered laconically.

Bill Anderson was out in the yard when Raines and Grat rode up. "You forget something, Grat?" he called jovially. "The way everybody packed in the liquor, I'm surprised you remembered to take your heads."

Raines's suspicions of the Hagens faded rapidly. Anderson had already verified the fact that the Hagens were there yesterday.

"Quint's got some questions he wants to ask," Grat said sourly.

Anderson stared quizzically at Raines. "Fire ahead," he invited.

"What time did the Hagens get here?"

"Shortly before noon. I know because I'd just told Ma that the first of the guests were due to arrive. A couple of minutes later, the Hagens were pounding on the door."

Grat spit in the dust, just missing Raines's boot, and his eyes were malicious.

Raines ignored the proffered insult. "What time did they leave?"

"You don't know the Hagens very well, or you'd know they never leave a party early. It was after midnight."

"Did they go out for any extended periods?"

"Only for the necessary trips, and they only lasted a few minutes."

Raines sighed. The Hagens had a solid alibi. Jessie's guesses were all wrong.

"If Bill here isn't enough," Grat growled, "I imagine I could dig up eighteen or twenty more people. All saying the same thing."

"Won't be necessary, Grat," Raines answered.

"Now, suppose you tell me what this has been all about," Grat demanded.

"I was looking for a murderer, Grat. Sometime yesterday, one of the Kilmers' herders was ambushed and a flock of sheep were run over a cliff."

Grat's face went tight, and there might have been a shade of fear in his eyes. "Jessie accused me?"

"He thought you could be behind this," Raines said gravely.

"Why, that damned liar," Grat exploded. "Did he claim he saw me?"

Raines shook his head.

"Because he didn't see me," Grat said hotly. "I was over here at the Andersons' during the time when that murder happened."

"That's been well-established," Raines said wearily. "I'm not laying any charge on you."

He started away, then stopped. "I know what a hothead you are, Grat. I suggest you drop it right here. Don't try seeking out Jessie to even things with him. He did lose a herder. I saw the body. Somebody did it. That puts everything on shaky ground. If some of the hotheads kick it around some more, the war could break out all over again. Grat," he pleaded, "can't you see that?"

"I see it," Grat growled. "I don't want you and that mealy-mouthed judge to go looking for me."

"We won't, Grat, if you avoid all semblance of trouble."

"What about Jessie?"

"He'll pull off, after I talk to him. He's walking a tightrope like you are."

"I don't even want my shadow to touch him," Grat said furiously.

"Good. Just keep it that way. I'll be riding back to the Kilmers'. Thank you, Mr. Anderson."

Anderson chuckled. "First time anybody thanked me for telling the truth."

Raines mounted and looked back. Anderson and Grat Hagen had their heads close together. Raines wished he could have heard that conversation. He didn't expect the story about Grat's whereabouts yesterday to be changed, but it would be interesting to hear their reaction.

He pulled up before the Kilmers' house and sat there a long moment. He faced a stormy session and knew it. Jessie would rave about him listening to a damned liar.

He sighed and swung off. Jessie must have seen him coming, for he was waiting at the door.

"You didn't arrest him?" Jessie asked in amazement.

Raines shook his head. "I could stand a cup of coffee." He proceeded past Jessie and walked into the kitchen. Asa greeted him with a frosty face. "Asa, I'd sure appreciate a cup of coffee."

Jessie came into the kitchen. "I'm not so sure you're worth it. Grandpa, he didn't arrest Grat."

"God Almighty," Asa howled. "You had purpose and motivation. What else did you need?"

"I needed witnesses." Raines glanced disapprovingly at Jessie. "Not just some wild guesses."

Jessie flushed. "You just let that liar talk his way out of this."

"Watch that kind of talk," Raines said sharply. "That could get your face busted."

"I knew it," Jessie groaned. "You listened to him and took everything he said as Gospel Truth."

"I listened to him," Raines said calmly. "Particularly when it was backed up by Bill Anderson. Grat said he could get twenty more people to swear that the Hagens spent yesterday there from noon to after midnight. The Hagens attended an anniversary party at the Andersons'."

The fury was diminishing in Jessie's eyes. He had never known Raines to lie about anything. He sank limply into a chair. "Do you believe him, Quint?" he asked hollowly.

"I do," Raines said firmly. "There's no other way to look at it."

"Sounds like Quint knows what he's talking about, son." Asa's face was calm. He accepted everything Raines said.

Jessie looked utterly defeated. "You saw Deke, Quint. You know he was shot."

"Positive of it." Raines's mouth was a thin line. "And I'm convinced that the Hagens had no hand in it."

Jessie's face was drawn. He was suffering. "It pointed that way," he said helplessly.

"Because in your mind you wanted it that way," Raines said relentlessly.

"This means you're giving up on Deke's murder?"

"*You* said that, Jessie. Not me. I'm going to wear my butt out trying to find out who was behind this."

"You sound like you don't have much hope in accomplishing that," Asa said caustically.

"It's going to take longer. I'll admit that." Raines shrugged. "I don't have the deputies I had before. I promise you one thing. Deke's murderers hadn't better rest easy." He held out a hand and slowly closed it. "This old claw is older and hasn't quite as much power. But it'll still work. Jessie, get that despairing look off your face. Keep your eyes peeled. Report anything you think suspicious to me. Those criminals will make a misstep." He stood and rolled his shoulders. "It ain't done yet. Thanks for the coffee." Raines grinned whimsically. "That thanks is about all you'll get right now. Asa, talk some sense into this hothead." He reset his hat and walked toward the door. He looked back from there. He didn't know how much good that little talk would do. Asa had been a pretty fair hothead himself. Neither of them looked up as he closed the door behind him.

CHAPTER 13

Three men sat around the dying cook fire inside the mouth of a cave. The cave cut off most of the chances of the fire being seen.

"I'd better go into town and get some more supplies," Curt said. "I'd like to find out if there's any talk about our raid against the Kilmers."

"You're coming back?" Young squalled in quick alarm. The week of inactivity had palled on all three of them. It showed the worst on Young.

"You know I'll be back," Curt replied. "Stay close until I return." There wasn't any use telling these two to try and get along. They couldn't let an hour pass without finding something new to bicker about.

"We won't leave this spot," Royal promised.

Curt nodded. He could depend on Royal. Young was another matter. He picked up his saddle. His horse was tethered in a little copse of trees a good three hundred yards away. Curt was well-pleased with himself. The chance of some passerby spotting the cave or tethered horses was small. He had no idea whose land they were on, but it was pretty damned isolated. Curt wanted to keep it that way. Of course, this kind of living was inconvenient, but it was a hell of a lot safer.

He was cursing softly when he finished the trudge to the copse of trees. The ground had been rocky, and a saddle weighed forty pounds, enough weight to pull at a man's arm and shoulder.

He leaned against the horse he had bought, and he'd be damned if the poor animal didn't seem happy to see him. Curt hadn't thought much about it, but he guessed animals could get lonesome too.

His breathing steadied, and he smoothed out the blanket and put on the saddle. This wasn't much of a horse, but Curt was grateful of one aspect. This horse didn't have enough spirit to resist saddling.

He finished and mounted. Young and Royal would have to see that their horses were moved tomorrow to get a little grazing. He whistled tunelessly as he rode. The sun was almost down, and it would probably be dark when he got to town. That suited him fine. He wanted to talk to Jacob, and it was just as well that nobody saw him go into the Keeley house.

Curt hadn't hurried his trip, and it was fully dark when he rode into town. He paused momentarily before the Keeley house. Ah, he thought in satisfaction. Only a single light was on in the house. Somebody was up.

He dismounted and led the horse down the side yard. Halfway down the house was a huge lilac bush. Curt remembered it from being a kid. It was too early for the bush to be in blossom, but memory captured it all for Curt. A month from now the bush would be covered with fragrant blossoms. Nostalgia reached from the past and yanked savagely at his mind. He had played around this bush when he was just a kid. A man didn't realize how much a bush could grow until he saw it like this.

He shook himself. There was nothing sentimental in him. He tied the horse to the bush, looked back and was satisfied. It would take a sharp eye to pick out the horse against the bush. Curt heard the sharp click of its teeth, as the animal went immediately to work nipping off the first small growth of the leaves. He grinned wickedly. That would probably make Jacob unhappy, and somehow that tickled Curt. He guessed there wasn't much brotherly love between them these days.

He moved back to the front door and rapped softly. Evidently, it wasn't loud enough for it to be heard, and he rapped with more vigor.

He was ready to knock again. This time he would arouse somebody. The door opened, and Jacob said in a tight, cautious voice, "Yes? Who is it?"

Curt's lips curled. What a poor little frightened man, living on the verge of absolute terror. "It's Curt," he said softly.

That frightened sound sounded a whole lot like a scared sheep. "I told you never to come here," Jacob said. His voice sounded tight and choked.

"I had to see you, Jacob. Are you going to ask me in, or do I just stand out here?"

Keeley unwillingly stepped out of the door. "Come in," he said churlishly. "Keep your voice down. Mrs. Larson has gone to bed, and I don't want her hearing you."

He led Curt into the parlor and closed the door behind them. Curt seated himself and said, "I could use a drink, Jacob."

There was pure distaste on Keeley's face, but he nodded. Curt grinned fiendishly. His brother was filled with the milk of human kindness. He opened a cabinet and produced a bottle and a glass.

"Aren't you drinking with me, Jacob?"

"I rarely drink," Keeley said stiffly.

Curt rolled the liquor around in his mouth. At least Jacob kept good whiskey on hand.

"What do you want?" Keeley repeated.

"I thought you'd be glad to see me by this time," Curt said reproachfully. "After what we did." There was no response, and Curt's eyebrows rose. "Don't tell me you haven't heard about it?"

"Oh, there's talk about it in town," Keeley said sourly. "You destroyed a few of the Kilmers' sheep."

"More than a few," Curt murmured. "We shot a herder in getting at them."

Keeley nodded. "I know. Raines has been all over town, asking about it. But you didn't hurt the Kilmers very badly."

Curt shook his head. "There never was much gratitude in you, Jacob. Here we risked our necks, and you show no more approval than that."

"I expected bigger results," Keeley said, his voice rising. "After the first raid, I expected you to hit them again and harder. Why, you hardly made a dent in them."

Curt frowned. The risk to him, Royal and Young meant nothing to his brother. "We laid low until we heard how people reacted to what happened."

Keeley saw that he had affronted Curt, and he said, "It aroused quite a bit of reaction. Everybody is talking about this being the start of the second war. It's helpful, but it doesn't do much good."

Curt laughed, a short burst of strident sound. "You thought we'd keep on hitting the Kilmers until they threw up their hands in surrender? Nothing works that fast."

The sense of Curt's words must have gotten through to Keeley, for he looked deflated. "What do you plan to do now, Curt?"

"Pick out a good-looking spot, Jacob. I don't believe in rushing into anything."

Keeley seemed suddenly beaten. "Sure, Curt, any way you want it."

Keeley was amenable, and this was the opportunity Curt sought.

"You remember I asked for six hundred dollars because I spent more for expenses than I expected?"

Keeley nodded, his face strained. "I remember," he muttered.

"I'd like to pick up that money while I'm here."

There was pure distress in Keeley's voice. "I don't carry that kind of money on me," he spluttered.

"How much do you have?" Curt pressed him.

"Maybe I could raise close to a hundred dollars in the house."

Curt studied him and was convinced Keeley was telling the truth. "Get it," he ordered.

Keeley left the room, and Curt grinned wolfishly when he was gone. He was dealing with a much weaker man than he realized.

Keeley came back and counted out ninety-eight dollars into Curt's hand. "That takes almost every dime I have here."

Curt grinned. "That'll do for right now." His voice hardened. "Don't forget you still owe me the rest of it."

Jacob couldn't meet Curt's eyes. Maybe it wasn't such a wise idea to pull him into his life.

The silence grew heavy, and Keeley finally asked, "What are your next plans?"

"We'll move again in a day or two," Curt said, a cruel smile touching his lips. "But on a much bigger scale. The next time I'll really hurt the Kilmers. They'll scream so loud you'll hear them all over the county."

Keeley wanted to ask what those plans were, then decided against it. Maybe it was wiser for him not to know any more about Curt's plans.

They sat there, the silence unbroken. Keeley was grateful when Curt finally got to his feet. "I'd better be going," Curt said. "I still have to pick up some supplies."

Keeley almost asked him to keep in touch, then reconsidered. The less he knew about what was going on, the better off he was.

"Good night, Curt," he said, his voice stiff.

Curt chuckled. "Good night, brother." What a mockery that term was.

CHAPTER 14

The closer Curt got to the cave's mouth, the unhappier he grew. Where in the hell were Royal and Young? He didn't object to one of them being asleep, but he didn't want both sleeping at the same time.

He ventured a cautious, "Hallo," and a voice answered from the shadows of the cave's entrance. "Yes?" Royal said.

"Did I wake you up?" Curt asked sarcastically.

Royal snorted. "I been watching you for the last couple of hundred yards. Asleep, hell."

Curt got down and untied the gunnybag from behind his saddle. "Well, it didn't look that way to me. Where's Young?"

"I guess he whimpered his way to sleep." Royal took the bag, and the movement produced a musical clinking from the sack. "You buy more liquor?"

"We were about out, weren't we?" Curt said. "Wake up Young. I want him to take my horse and tether him. He can bring back the saddle."

Royal grinned wickedly. "He'll complain his head off. All that weight and all that walking."

"Get him," Curt snapped.

Young was rubbing the last of the sleep from his eyes when he reached Curt.

"Why me?" he whined. "I always got to do all the errands."

"Why *not* you?" Curt said hotly. "I made the trip into town." He handed Young the reins and watched him shuffle off. "He sounds like he's working his butt off," he commented. "I'm kinda sorry I asked him in."

"I'm damned sorry," Royal said tersely. He was pawing through the gunnybag and setting its contents on the ground. "You bought four bottles," he chortled. "Look at all this food. And Young bellyaches. He hasn't had it this good for a long time."

He stretched out on the ground and uncorked a bottle. He took a long pull and said contentedly, "This ain't a bad life. Plenty of food and whiskey and not much work. There's only one thing lacking." He handed the bottle to Curt.

"What's that?" Curt asked. He was sure Royal would say, "Women."

"An occasional bath."

Curt nodded. Dirt kept accumulating on a man until he was encrusted with it. He took another small drink. This was good liquor, going down smoothly without a vicious jolt to a man's system. "That and some clean clothes," he said. "If it gets unbearable, you can always jump in a creek."

Royal shivered. "At this time of year? I can stand myself for a while. Did you see the boss?" He didn't know who the boss was, and he was wise enough not to ask.

"What makes you ask that?"

Royal chuckled. "We weren't that low on food to make it necessary to go into town."

Curt grinned. Royal was canny enough to figure out that the boss was in Landers. "I saw him."

"He satisfied with what we've done so far?"

"Nope," Curt answered laconically. "He wants more done."

"Ain't that typical of a boss?" Royal groused. "He sure must have a hatred for the Kilmers to go after them like this."

"Maybe he has," Curt replied. "I never asked him." How Royal's eyebrows would go up if he knew the boss was Curt's brother.

"Did he have any plans?" Royal asked impatiently.

"He wants us to really hit the Kilmers. What we did didn't make a dent in them."

"Could you satisfy him?"

"I think I did," Curt answered calmly. "It took some doing. That little bunch we destroyed was just a starter. The grass is coming on. The Kilmers will be sending out bigger flocks. The wagons will go with them. A herder will be driving each wagon. They'll go farther and stay out longer."

Royal sucked on his teeth as he turned what Curt said over in his mind. He spat and said, "There was a herder with that bunch we took care of."

"I know. We knew what we had to do to get rid of him."

"I kinda enjoyed that," Royal said reflectively.

"I thought you did," Curt answered. There was a vicious streak in Royal. He would hate to be on opposite sides of him.

Young came up then, and he was limping badly. He groaned as

he laid down the saddle. He took a tentative step and let out a string of oaths.

"What's eating you?" Royal asked unfeelingly.

"I stepped on a stone in the dark and fell. I think I've twisted my ankle."

"Going or coming?" Royal asked.

"On the way back," Young answered sullenly. He was suspicious that Royal wasn't really sympathetic.

"Then you were lucky," Royal said solemnly.

"I don't think I was so lucky."

"Sure you were. You could have tripped on the way there. That would have meant a lot longer way to walk on that sore ankle."

Young stared in outraged dignity, then he choked out a "Go to hell."

Royal cackled as Young limped into the cave.

"Royal, you shouldn't ride him so hard," Curt said.

Royal reached for the bottle. "Aw, he makes me sick. Always complaining."

Curt waited until Royal handed him the bottle, drank, then rose. "I'd better see how bad his ankle is. He could have busted a bone."

Young was stretched out at the far end of the cave. Curt offered him the bottle. "This might ease it a little."

Young drank, then gagged. He choked off a groan. "That big ox makes me sick. Always thinks I'm faking."

"How bad is it, Young?" Curt knelt beside him. He couldn't see too well, and he let his fingers see for him. He pressed them against the ankle, and Young yelped.

"Damn it, that hurt."

"Sure, it did," Curt said consolingly. The boot felt tight in that area. There must be some swelling in that ankle.

"Young, we'd better get that boot off. If it swells more, we'll have to cut it off in the morning."

Young blew out a breath, and it sounded like a squeak. "Take it easy, will you?"

"I will." Curt backed up to Young, and Young thrust the booted foot between his legs. Curt gripped the boot by heel and toe and tried to remove it gently. There must be quite an amount of swelling, for the boot didn't budge. "I'm going to have to yank on it. Hang on."

He exerted all his pressure, and the boot began to slip off Young's foot.

"Oh, Jesus Christ," Young yelled. "I thought you were going to yank my foot off."

"I know it hurt." Curt laid the boot beside Young and knelt to more closely inspect the ankle. He struck a match, and in the feeble light he could make out the puffiness there.

"It's swollen pretty bad, Young." Curt's fingers pressed gently against the puffiness. "I'm no doctor, but I don't think you broke any bones. You'd better stay off it for a few days."

Young tried to control his voice, but it came out high and squeaky. "I guess I'll have to."

Curt looked curiously at him, but he couldn't see his face plainly in the darkness. Young sounded as though he was hurting bad.

"I'll whittle you out a crutch so you can get around," Curt said and moved back to where Royal lay.

"What was he squealing about, Curt?"

"He wasn't faking, Royal. He's got at the least a bad sprain."

That didn't touch Royal at all. "Tough," he said.

"He won't be able to get around on it for several days."

Royal swore in disgust. "You mean he's going to hold us here during that time?"

Curt shook his head. "We're going ahead tomorrow. The two of us can do it. But I've got to make a crutch so he can get around."

"You do it," Royal said churlishly. "I'm too tired to take on any extra chores."

"I intended to," Curt said evenly. He moved out of the cave and selected a tree some fifty yards away. He wished he had better light to work with, but waiting for morning could cost Young unnecessary pain. He found a fork in the branch and it took quite a bit of whittling to shape it into the form he wanted. He trimmed off the end of the stick and left the final cutting as to the length until he measured it with Young's height.

His hand was sore when he finished. It wasn't a fancy job, but Young should be able to get around on it.

He carried the crutch back to the cave, and Royal was asleep. That suited Curt just fine. He carried his crude crutch back to where Young lay. Young was asleep too. Curt decided to let him sleep. The final fitting could go until daylight. Young had to be in some pain. Getting to sleep was an accomplishment for him. Curt turned and moved softly away. He went back to Royal and sat down beside him.

"Didn't he appreciate your crutch?" Royal asked unexpectedly.

"I didn't ask him, Royal. He was asleep." Curt couldn't tell what Royal's grunt meant.

"Hanging around here a few more days will drive me nuts," Royal said passionately.

"That's one of the reasons I worked on Young's crutch. We're taking off tomorrow morning. Just where we left off. I won't have to be concerned about Young not being able to move around."

"Leaving him alone will probably scare the hell out of him," Royal said. He stretched out and in a few moments was asleep. Royal didn't have anything on his conscience, for his snoring was regular.

CHAPTER 15

The cells behind Raines's office must be empty, for there was nobody in the office. Jessie got up again, for the twelfth time, and walked to the window. He badly wanted to talk to Raines, and it looked as though he wouldn't be able to today. Raines was out somewhere tending to what Jessie didn't know.

He made one more trip to the window and said an explosive, "Damn. It's about time." Raines was just tying up at the tie rack. Jessie stood while Raines crossed the walk and entered the office. Raines's shoulders were slumped, and his face was heavy with fatigue.

"Hello, Quint," Jessie said quietly.

Raines let a nod speak for him. He was in a bad mood, and it showed in his first words. "Don't you go ajumping all over me, Jessie. I got no news for you. I've wore my butt thin trying to cover this county all at once. I couldn't count up all the cattlemen I've talked to. All of them deny any involvement. Most of them have solid alibis." He sat down behind his desk, and his head lowered. "Lord, how long has it been since I've had a good night's sleep?"

Jessie had come in here determined to raise hell with Raines. But the man's apparent fatigue got through to him, and he felt a sympathy for the harassed sheriff. He settled into a chair opposite the desk. "How do you figure it, Quint?"

Quint held his head in both hands, and Jessie wondered if he did that to ease a splitting headache. "I can't figure a thing, Jessie. All I can possibly see is that some outsider just happened through your place, killed Deke, stampeded your sheep, then skedaddled when he stopped to think what he had done. But that doesn't make sense. What good would it have done him unless he's a plumb crazy man. Wouldn't that be pure hell if we found out we're looking for a crazy man?"

Jessie shook his head. Raines hadn't convinced him at all. "Somebody had a sound reason behind this, Quint. Find out the reason, and you can put your thumb on your man. I still think—"

Raines sighed and cut him short. "I know what you think. You still believe the Hagens were involved in this. Lord, Jessie, you're one stubborn man."

Jessie flushed. "They've got a solid reason to be behind this. My fight with Grat stirred up all the old hatred. The Hagens waited until they saw a good opportunity. They took it."

"My God, Jessie," Raines said in wonder. "You never let go of a thought once you get it in your head. I'm satisfied that the Hagens had no part in this."

Jessie's patience was wearing thin. Raines was an obdurate man. He was guilty of the same thing he accused Jessie of. He closed his mind to any new thought.

Jessie took a step toward the door and stopped. "I'm telling you this, Quint. We sent all the flocks out yesterday. The herders took the wagons with them. They'll be a considerable distance from the house. Isolated and alone," he finished grimly. "More vulnerable than ever before. If that unknown wants another crack at us, he'll never have a better opportunity."

Raines's face was a dull red. Jessie was accusing him of laxness without saying it. "I'm doing everything I can, Jessie."

"It better be," Jessie said flatly. He started for the door, and Raines stopped him.

"Jessie, you armed all your herders and told them what to look for?"

"Do you think I'm stupid?" Jessie asked hotly. "They're armed with rifles and handguns with plenty of ammunition for both guns." He stopped and pointed an accusing finger at Raines. "I'm telling you this, Quint. If something happens to one of my flocks or its herder, I'm holding you solely responsible."

For an instant, Raines was so angry his vision swam. What did Jessie think he was, a miracle worker? Then he regained control. Jessie had every right to his attitude. "I wouldn't blame you, Jessie. All I can tell you right now is to keep a sharp eye out. Report anything that seems the least out of the ordinary. Tell your herders to keep their eyes peeled."

"I already have," Jessie said grimly. "If they spot anything suspicious, they'll shoot first and ask questions later." He spun and stalked out of the office.

Raines sat there a long moment, his face deeply troubled. He may have a new war on his hands, and somebody could be readily hurt.

Arm a bunch of nervous, jumpy men and take away all restrictions meant that lead would fly. The most innocent of people crossing the Kilmers' land could easily draw a hurried reprisal. One killing could lead to others. This whole damned county could explode before his eyes. Oh Lord! He was so damned weary. He felt like putting his head down on his arms and bawling. He straightened and chased the weakness away. All he could do was to look harder and faster. Yes, and with more efficient hunting, he thought.

Curt was awake at the first dawn. He walked back to where Young slept and stood watching him. Young's sleep hadn't been soothing. He rolled in his sleep and mumbled vague, incomprehensible words. Curt shook his head. Young looked so immature and helpless. Curt had a sense of unease. He wished he hadn't asked Young to join them.

He leaned over and gently shook Young awake. For a moment, Young fought the intruding hand. He slapped at it, and his face was stamped with terror.

"Easy, Young. It's me."

Sanity returned to Young's eyes, and he sat up, his face stricken. "I didn't know it was you, Curt. I had such bad dreams. The ankle gave me hell all night."

"I understand, Young. Let me look at that ankle again."

It looked worse in the daylight. The ankle was swollen far worse than when he had first seen it. Now vivid blacks and blues and yellows were streaking the flesh. Curt didn't know whether or not Young had broken a bone.

"Let me help you up, Young."

"What for?" Young replied sullenly. "I can't walk anyplace."

Curt bent over and picked up the crude crutch. Young apparently hadn't seen it until now. "I know that, Young. That's why I whittled this out for you."

Young was in an ungracious mood. "It won't help me any."

Curt was more level-headed than Royal, but he was losing his patience. "You can try, can't you?" he asked shortly. "I want to see if the length is right."

With Curt's help, Young struggled to his feet. He stood on one foot and leaned against Curt's shoulder. Curt measured the crutch up against him. Just as he thought last night, the crutch was about a foot too long.

He leaned Young against the cave wall, and Young protested shrilly, "I can't stand on one foot. The ankle's killing me."

"You can stand for a minute or so. It won't take me any longer." He opened up the pocketknife and set to whittling a foot off of the crutch. He didn't know what kind of wood he had picked in the darkness, but it was tough. He took a small chip out at a time, working around the limb. It finally was weakened enough for him to snap it off. He spent a moment longer smoothing the rough end.

"Try this," he said, handing the crutch to Young.

Young took a tentative step. "It still hurts," he complained.

"But you can get around, can't you?"

The sharpness in Curt's voice made Young hang his head. "I guess so," he mumbled. "But what do I want to get around for?"

"To take care of yourself," Curt said brusquely.

That widened Young's eyes, and terror returned to them. "You're leaving me?" he cried.

"For a couple of days. Damn it, Young. We've got to do the work we promised. You'll be all right here. I'm leaving you plenty of food. When we get back, you'll be able to get around better."

The pleading in Young's eyes made him sick. Royal was right. There was a pure streak of baby in the man. Curt tried to hide the disgust he felt and asked, "Want to try the crutch a little more to get used to it?"

"You can't leave me alone," Young pleaded. "You can see I'm almost helpless. What if something happened to me?"

"Just see that it doesn't," Curt snapped.

He walked to the front of the cave, and Royal asked, "What was all that jawing about?"

"Young doesn't want us to leave him."

Royal grinned twistedly. "Something happened in prison to that boy. He wasn't like that before he went in. Prison knocked all the toughness out of him."

"I wish I'd realized it before I asked him to join us," Curt growled. "What the hell can happen to him?"

"Nothing," Royal answered promptly. "Unless he takes unnecessary chances. Knowing him, I doubt that."

"Going now, Young," Curt called back.

His lips twisted at the lack of response. "Still sulking," he murmured.

"Won't do him any good," Royal said and chuckled. "Is he faking that bad ankle?"

Curt shook his head. "No, he isn't. It was badly swollen this morning. I can't tell if it's broken."

Royal chuckled. "Well, time will prove which it is."

"It'll do that all right," Curt said soberly. What would they do if time proved that Young had a much more serious injury than just a sprain? He shrugged away the disquieting thoughts. There was nothing he could do about it now.

They rode for half a day, taking it slowly and cautiously. From every high prominence they surveyed the country, only moving when they were satisfied that the country was empty.

"I think we're back on Kilmer land," Curt said as they paused again.

"What are you looking for?"

"A flock of sheep and its herder."

"Are you going to try the same thing we used the first time?"

"I doubt it. The land there lent itself to our purpose. We won't be so lucky again."

It was midafternoon when Curt threw up a hand, stopping Royal. "I think I hear sheep."

Royal's face was screwed up as he listened. "I don't hear anything."

Curt wouldn't be swerved. "It came from up ahead. We'd better check it out on foot."

He dismounted and tied his horse to a pine sapling. He waited until Royal did the same, then the two moved slowly ahead. The ground tilted sharply upward, and before they reached the crest, Curt was beginning to feel the strain in his legs.

"Ah," he said in relief as the tremble in his legs stopped. What he saw gave him tremendous satisfaction. A flock of sheep far greater than the flock they destroyed was grazing before him. He couldn't tell how many they were, but they had to be in the hundreds. They moved slowly to the west, busy with their grazing. A herder plodded behind them, a dog trotting at his side. Every now and then, the dog seemed to sense a break by one of the sheep, for he was off on a barking run, cutting off the sheep's threatened break, yapping and snapping at its heels until it gave up its plan of escape, quickly turning and trotting back to the main body of the flock.

"That dog works damned good," Royal remarked in a low voice. "Sure saves that herder many a step."

"He couldn't handle those sheep without the dog," Curt grunted. They watched for the better part of an hour, only moving when the flock threatened to put too much distance between them and the animals.

"I don't see what good this is doing us," Royal said in a disgruntled voice.

"The day's about over," Curt remarked. "I imagine the herder will be taking them back to where he intends to spend the night."

Royal's face brightened. "Then you plan to do something there."

Curt grinned. "You're getting brighter. I sure don't plan to do anything now. Ah," he said in satisfaction. "Look! The dog is begging to turn them."

On a command from the herder and a waving of his arm, the dog started turning the flock. He got them going in the direction he wanted and again fell in beside the herder. The herder reached down and patted the dog's head.

"They're damned close, ain't they, Curt?"

"You'd be too, if you only had the dog to rely on," Curt replied. He reached out and checked Royal's motion to rise. "Not so fast. We know the direction they're taking. We can't get too close now."

"Why not?" Royal queried.

"The wind is blowing across us to the herder and dog. With that sensitive nose, the dog will pick us up the moment we get too close. We'll follow them to the night's camp and decide what to do then."

"You know a hell of a lot about sheep," Royal grunted.

"A little," Curt admitted. "Not as much as that herder does."

They spent the rest of the afternoon following the flock. Well up ahead, Curt caught a glimpse of a strange-looking wagon. "That looks like where the night's camp will be. I'd say the herder has used the site before."

Curt changed their direction so that the wind blew in their faces. "We're upwind of the dog now," he said. "I'd feel a lot safer if the dog doesn't spot us."

"You're sure taking a lot of caution," Royal growled. "There's only one herder and two of us."

"That herder's got a gun," Curt pointed out.

"So what?" Royal asked obstinately. "One bullet stops him."

Curt shook his head. Royal was a fire-eater, plunging ahead recklessly. It never hurt to take precautions and look things over. Besides, it was still light. Light would never work to the advantage of what he had in mind.

They lay and watched the sheep corralled for the night.

"You mean that flimsy little barrier will hold them?" Royal asked.

Curt nodded. "It will, if the sheep aren't unduly disturbed. Ah, the herder's taking the dog inside. Probably going to feed him. He'll turn him out later."

Curt was right. A half hour later, the door to the hut opened and the herder reappeared. He stooped and patted the dog, then put him outdoors.

That dog knew his business. He made round after round of the corral, barking occasionally at something he didn't like.

"What's he barking for?" Royal asked irritably.

The waiting was beginning to pall on Curt. "How in the hell would I know? Probably smells something that disturbs him."

"Us?" Royal asked.

Curt shook his head. "I don't think so. If he smelled us, he'd raise a lot more hell than just a bark now and then." He stiffened as the wind changed direction. It now blew away from them.

Royal noticed the change in Curt's attitude. "Now what's the matter?"

"Wind changed on us. We'd better move. The wind's carrying our scent directly to the dog."

It was too late. The keen nose of the dog had caught something alien in the wind. He charged around the corral and headed directly toward where the men lay. He was barking furiously.

"Shut him up," Curt said tersely.

He thought Royal would never stop aiming. With each passing second, the dog drew closer. Royal finally pulled the trigger. By his following curse, Curt knew he had missed.

Royal fired again. The dog went down as suddenly as though it had slammed into a stone wall. He yelped once more, then was silent.

"Got him," Royal said, the boast big in his voice. "If you think that was an easy shot—"

"Tell me about it later," Curt interrupted. His attention was focused on the hut's door. The herder should have heard those shots. He should be coming out to investigate.

The minutes dragged away, and the door didn't open. "What's he doing?" Curt fretted.

"Maybe he's playing it smart," Royal replied. "Trying to catch us off guard." His rifle had never wavered from the hut's door. "He'll show anytime now."

Curt still fretted. It was getting darker every passing second. It was getting harder to pick out the door from the blob of the hut.

"We'd better move closer, Royal. With the dog gone, it'll be safer."

They crawled a hundred yards nearer the hut. "Can you see the door now?" Curt asked.

"Good enough," Royal answered. Strain was beginning to show in his voice. "He didn't hear those shots, or he's trying to outwait us."

The door suddenly opened, and a figure made a dash for the steps. The figure was wearing a white shirt, and the flash of it was enough to pick him out.

"Do you see him?" Curt asked in a tight voice.

"I see him." Royal's voice had calmed down. He enjoyed action of this kind.

The figure ran some twenty yards from the hut when Royal squeezed the trigger. It was followed quickly by a second shot. The running figure suddenly collapsed. "Got him," Royal said, wicked satisfaction in his voice.

"Keep your rifle on him," Curt advised as he got to his feet. The figure hadn't moved again, but the man had played it shrewd by not rushing out of the hut at the sound of the shots. He could be faking again. "Shoot if he moves, Royal," Curt ordered.

They cautiously approached the figure. Curt hadn't taken his eyes off him. He blew out a long breath as he surveyed the limp figure. The man hadn't moved after Royal had hit him.

Royal toed him over. "Do you know him, Curt?"

"Never saw him before in my life."

Royal squatted for a closer look at the face. "Looks like a Mexican to me. I didn't think they ever came this far north."

"This one did," Curt remarked.

"Well, he ain't going anyplace else," Royal replied cynically.

"We'd better get our work done and get out of here," Curt said. He was nervously looking about.

"Something eating on you, Curt?"

"A rifle shot can travel a long way in this country. Somebody could have heard it."

"Naw," Royal said indulgently. "Show me what you want done."

The two men approached the flimsy corral. "Damnedest thing I ever saw," Royal remarked as he saw the corral up close. "This is nothing but some kind of cloth."

"Enough to hold sheep," Curt said. He went along the corral wall, kicking huge rents in the muslin. Royal followed his example.

Inside the corral the sheep were going wild. As either man approached, they dashed to the far side of the corral.

"What the hell's wrong with them?" Royal asked.

"They recognize us as strangers," Curt replied. "In a moment they'll find the holes and be gone."

Royal pointed his rifle at the sky. "I can hurry them up some."

"No more firing," Curt said sharply. "I told you how sound carries. Do you want to look up and see a bunch of hot-eyed horsemen coming at us?"

Royal grinned. "I can do without that."

Curt stepped inside the corral, and Royal followed him. The sheep darted away from them.

"They look like they don't want to leave," Royal remarked.

"This is familiar to them. Keep pressing them."

Each man advanced, waving his arms. A solid wall of sheep hit the torn and weakened muslin. They crashed through it, bleating frantically. In a moment the darkness swallowed them up.

"You tell me what good that did," Royal said. "They'll just gather them up in the morning."

"Not very many," Curt said cynically. "They'll run until they're exhausted. By that time, wolves and coyotes will discover they're out. They'll cut the numbers down until there won't be many left to gather. Let's get moving. We've got a long way to where we left our horses."

He looked back after a dozen steps. The scene was quiet and peaceful. A casual glance could tell that a dead man lay there, but all the sheep were gone. It wouldn't be undiscovered for long. All hell would break loose when the owner discovered his loss.

CHAPTER 16

Raines and Jessie rode in tight-lipped silence. Not a word had passed between them in the last ten miles. There had been enough angry words when Jessie first burst into Raines's office. Raines had never seen a wilder, more angry man. For the first few seconds, the words had poured out so fast that Raines hadn't been able to understand them.

He finally got Jessie slowed down enough to make sense out of what he was saying. "Those murderous bastards killed Mendoza last night," Jessie said. "Sure, I'm sure. I was out there the first thing this morning. They killed his dog too. Mendoza had gotten some twenty yards from his hut before he was cut down."

The muscles in Raines's face had gone rigid, making his cheekbones stand out starkly. "I promise you one thing, Jessie, I'll run the bushwhackers down."

"That promise isn't worth very much," Jessie had replied bitterly. "You don't even have an idea of where to look."

Raines hadn't responded to that bitter retort. A layman didn't understand the long, dogged work of the law.

"I'm thinking mostly of Mendoza," Jessie had gone on. "He was one of the most gentle men I've ever known. But I can't overlook the loss of my sheep."

"How many do you figure it was, Jessie?"

Jessie had thrown up his hands in angry futility. "I only know that we had close to two thousand head with Mendoza. The corral was busted all to pieces. If the bastards didn't run those sheep out, the sheep took advantage of the openings to run." His eyes closed briefly in anguish, and Raines knew he was reliving that horrible scene.

"That meant that those sheep were out all night with no dog or herder to protect them. The wolves and coyotes had a picnic. I can't tell you how many carcasses I looked at this morning."

"Any recovery, Jessie?"

"Maybe a couple of dozen. A few more might be found later this morning, but I'm not counting on it."

Jessie had every right to be furious. "I'm going out there with you, Jessie."

Jessie put a withering look on him. "I expected you to, Quint."

That had been the last of their conversation until this moment. "You didn't find tracks of any kind, Jessie?"

"I found some boot tracks. No horse tracks."

"How did you read them?"

"I think they left their horses and walked in," Jessie answered. "Two sets of boot tracks. I found where they stopped and watched Mendoza's hut." Jessie pursed his lips, then blew out a long breath. "You're supposed to be the expert on this. That's why I went after you."

Jessie was in a touchy temper this morning, and Raines couldn't blame him. The way events were going, they were crushing Jessie with tremendous weight.

They didn't speak anymore until the sheepherder's wagon came into view. Three men lounged outside it. "I brought them from the house," Jessie said.

Raines nodded to them, and the three gave him blank stares in turn. Damn it, Raines thought heatedly. They look like I'm the enemy.

"I told them to leave Mendoza here," Jessie said coldly, "until you got here. I wanted you to see it just like I found it."

Raines looked at the dead dog and man. Damn it, how he wished those inanimate bodies could talk. He needed all the help he could get.

"What do you make of it, Quint?"

Raines looked back at the hut, his eyebrows knitted. "Looks like he made a run for it," he speculated.

Jessie nodded. "My figuring exactly. I think he heard the shot that killed the dog, but he was smart enough not to make a quick dash for it. He waited until he thought things had quieted down." There was a choked sound in his voice. "He didn't wait long enough."

Jessie was suffering. Raines could catch it in every word Jessie said and in the deep lines in his face.

"This is where the corral was?"

"Where it *should* have been," Jessie said in a muffled tone. "You can see where they kicked or tore big holes in it."

He walked with Raines to the sorry remains of the corral. Most of it was down. Several long pieces of muslin were still attached to the stakes, and they flapped in the wind.

"You think the sheep broke for it, Jessie?"

"I think they were chased out," Jessie said savagely. "Strangers going into the corral would have driven the sheep crazy. Once they were on the run, nothing could have stopped them."

"You didn't find any of them?"

"As I told you, a couple of dozen head. Lots of bodies where the wolves and coyotes brought them down." Jessie turned the air blue with his swearing.

Raines waited patiently until Jessie ran down. Jessie had every right to use all the profanity that came to his mind.

Raines lifted his head. "Somebody coming, Jessie," he warned.

Jessie had heard the muted shouts, and he turned his head in that direction. It took several minutes for four men to appear from the south. They drove some twenty head of sheep.

"I brought every man I could spare," Jessie explained.

Raines nodded. He felt sick for Jessie. There had to be more sheep left out of the original flock.

"That all?" Jessie asked grimly.

One of the men nodded. "We ranged as far as we dared, Jessie. We thought we'd better bring this little bunch back. We found them huddled in a grove of trees." He shook his head in disbelief. "My God! The way the wolves and coyotes tore the rest to pieces. Everywhere we looked, we found plenty of evidence of what they'd done."

Jessie had iron control. Such a disaster could mean only financial ruin, but he never showed a trace of it. "Take them back to the house," Jessie ordered. "Tell Asa what happened. I'll be in shortly."

Raines waited until the four men moved off, driving the sheep. "You got something in mind?"

"You're damned right I have," Jessie said violently. "Who else would want to see the Kilmers hurt? They sure accomplished it yesterday."

"You talking about the Hagens again?"

"I am," Jessie shouted.

"That's only guessing again, Jessie."

"This time I'm going to prove it," Jessie said, his face flushed. "I'm riding over and accusing the Hagens to their faces. They'll show some signs of guilt. Nothing you can do will stop me."

Raines sighed. "I know that, but I'm going with you."

They rode the distance to the Hagens' house in utter silence. Both men stopped outside the clapboard house, and Jessie stared broodingly at it. "For a long time they've wanted to see us run out of the country. They succeeded last night." He raised his voice. "Hagens," he bawled, "I want to talk to all of you."

Grat came out first, followed by his younger brother, then his father. "What's all the yelling about?" Grat demanded.

"Where were you Hagens yesterday?" Jessie asked. He couldn't keep the quiver out of his voice.

Grat eyed him levelly. "I don't see where that's any of your business."

Jessie was ready to explode. "Easy, Jessie," Raines said in a low tone.

Jessie put bleak eyes on him, then looked back at Grat. "It's my business when my property's hurt."

"What the hell are you talking about?" Grat demanded.

"You tell him, Quint," Jessie ordered.

"Jessie had a herder shot yesterday and almost an entire flock destroyed."

That hit Grat hard. His mouth sagged open, and his eyes widened. "And he thinks we're to blame," he finally managed to say.

"Yes," Jessie said flatly.

Old man Hagen was the first to recover from the accusation. "No way," he howled. "Grat and Gary and me were busy all day yesterday moving a herd of cattle."

"Bull," Jessie said fiercely.

All three of the Hagens' faces were agitated. "We had six of our riders with us. Ask them if you're too thick-headed to believe us," Wirt said.

"It's up to you, Jessie," Raines said. "I'll have Wirt get those riders out here if you want."

Jessie shook his head. His face was bitter. "It wouldn't do any good. They all work for the Hagens. They'd lie for them."

"Why, goddamn you," Grat said and started forward.

"That's far enough," Raines said sternly.

"He still thinks we did it," Grat objected.

"You and I can't do anything about what Jessie thinks," Raines said. "Ready to go, Jessie?"

Jessie nodded dumbly. On the way back, Raines said, "I was afraid you were going to push it further. Your accusation wouldn't have stood up in any court."

Jessie raked him with fierce eyes. "They may have fooled you, but they didn't fool me. It was written all over their faces. They were as guilty as sin."

Raines's face was hopeless. "You'll never let the old hatred die, will you, Jessie?"

"Every time something happens, they've got a convenient alibi. It always gets them by, but it doesn't help me any. Why, damn it, they've ruined the Kilmers."

"I'll keep looking," Raines said awkwardly. "I can promise you—"

That was the fuse that exploded Jessie's temper. "I don't want any of your worthless promises. I'll do my own looking."

Raines pointed a finger at him, and his expression was bleak. "I'm warning you, Jessie. If your thick-headedness gets you into trouble you can't get out of, it'll go hard on you."

"Go to hell," Jessie cried and spurred ahead.

CHAPTER 17

"Another successful day," Curt said as he stripped the saddle off his horse. "We didn't see a soul on the way back. You know what that means?"

"No, what does it mean?" Royal asked. He was in an unpleasant mood, for he hadn't spoken once on the way back to the cave. To a direct question he might answer with a grunt.

"What's eating you?" Curt asked. "You sound like everything went wrong. It didn't; everything went right."

"I guess I'm getting tired of living like this," Royal said reflectively. "Living like animals in a cave."

Curt eyed him keenly. "What's different? You acted as though you enjoyed it before." He wasn't wrong in that statement. That killer streak in Royal had surfaced strongly on both their raids against the Kilmers.

"I enjoyed the killing part," Royal said frankly. "But what happens now? We sit around another week before we go into action again?"

"Maybe not," Curt replied. He finished stripping the bridle off his horse and slung the saddle over his shoulder. He started for the cave.

"Maybe living around that Young is getting on my nerves," Royal said. "I'm so damned tired of his complaining, I don't know how much longer I can stand it."

"I'm going into town tonight," Curt said, "to find out if the boss wants us to continue. You can stand Young that much longer, can't you?"

"I don't know," Royal said dubiously. "I just don't know."

They came in sight of the cave's mouth, and Royal said, "I wonder where Young is."

"Maybe inside," Curt remarked indifferently. "He won't have gone very far with that ankle."

"Hey, Young," Royal yelled. "Young."

"Why don't you yell it to the whole county that we're here?" Curt asked sarcastically.

Royal looked astonished at him. "Hell, there's nobody within miles of us."

"You *hope* there isn't," Curt corrected. "Somebody might just be passing close enough to hear you. He just might investigate who was doing all that yelling."

"You're beginning to sound more like Young every day," Royal said sulkily.

"And you're getting nastier-tempered every day," Curt replied. Here now, he admonished himself. Each personality was begging to rub on the other. They'd have to make a special effort to keep those tempers down until this job was over and they separated for good.

"Funny we don't see Young," Curt remarked. They were at the cave's mouth, and there was still no sight of Young. "Wonder where he could have gone," Curt pondered.

"It couldn't have been far," Royal said indifferently. "If he doesn't come back, it's no big loss."

Curt's eyebrows went up, but he kept his mouth shut. They were at the bickering point now. A little more, and it could easily break out into violent quarreling.

He waited until he was inside the cave before he dared speak a little louder. "Young," he called. "Are you in here?"

He had to adjust his eyes to the cave's shadowy interior. He thought he saw movement at the far end, and he hurried forward.

"Young," he said, anger rising in his voice as he saw the man cowering in a corner. "Didn't you hear me?"

"I heard you," Young said petulantly.

"Why didn't you answer me? I was getting worried about you."

"The hell you were," Young said, his voice getting shriller. "You two don't give a damn what happened to me. You went off and left me alone."

Royal came up in time to hear the last few words. "Oh, my God," he said in disgust. "He's at it again."

"Stop it, both of you," Curt ordered. "How's the ankle, Young?"

"A lot you care," Young answered. He was almost at the screaming point. "I ran out of firewood and had to eat the last two meals cold."

"I don't believe this," Royal said, amazement in his voice. "There's firewood in those trees less than a hundred yards from the cave. Curt left you a crutch. There's an ax."

"I tried using that crutch," Young said sullenly. "It hurt too much to walk with it. I was sure I couldn't swing the ax only on one foot."

"So you just gave up," Royal sneered. "What would have happened to you if we didn't come back?"

"I don't know—" Young started.

"That's enough," Curt said, raising his voice. "This has got to stop. If it doesn't, we'll be at each other's throats."

"Blame *him*," Young said doggedly. "He's always on me."

Royal's hands bunched, and Curt said, "That's enough, Royal. I mean it. How's the ankle, Young?"

"It hurts like hell," Young replied sullenly. "It never gives me any peace."

"Ain't that a shame?" Royal asked mockingly. "Poor little brave man. All he can do is suffer and bear it."

"I said, Stop it," Curt said furiously.

"Tell him," Young shouted. "He's always picking at me."

"Royal," Curt snapped, stopping Royal's reply. "Help me get some firewood, and we'll get a fire going. Maybe some warm food will change both of you."

"Can't you see where this is going?" he asked Royal as he finished felling a small dead tree. He chopped the tree into more usable lengths. Between strokes he said, "Keep it up, and you two will be trying to shoot each other."

"I'd like to see him try it," Royal said viciously. "Nothing would give me more pleasure than to shut him up forever."

"What would that accomplish?" Curt asked. The agreement between them was falling apart before his eyes. He doubted, the way things were going, that they'd be able to stand each other long enough to finish the job Jacob wanted done. His eyes widened as a thought occurred to him. "I've got an idea how everybody can benefit." He shook his head at Royal's questions. "No, I'll tell you after we get a meal fixed."

He got the fire started and dumped the contents of three cans into a pan. He held the pan over the flames, coughing a couple of times over the smoke swirling lazily in the air. Living in a cave wasn't the best in the world. The ventilation wasn't good enough, and it didn't carry off the smoke.

He distributed the contents of the pan among them and asked, "How would you two like to get an extra thousand dollars apiece?"

That caught their attention. Royal set down his plate and said, "That could make it bearable enough to stand living with him." His eyes narrowed in suspicion. "I knew you were making more money than you let on. So you decided it was worthwhile to give us a bigger cut?"

It took effort for Curt to keep his face composed. "I didn't get any extra money. But I can talk to the boss and see if I can't pry a few more dollars out of him. I'm not promising anything," he warned. "He might be satisfied with what's already been done. I'd have to talk to him. I'll ride into town and see how he stands. But only on one condition," he cautioned. "You two will have to get along. Do you understand that?"

The thought of that extra money put a gleam in Royal's eyes. "For that amount of money, I could force myself to stand him."

"Young?" Curt questioned.

Young wouldn't look at Royal. "If he stays off me, I guess I could go along."

Curt had to fight his temper back. It was pure hell living with these two. "All right," he conceded. "I'll ride in today. If I find out you two argued while I've been gone, forget about any additional money."

Royal gave him a crooked grin. "There won't be any arguing. I won't talk to him."

"Do you think that makes me unhappy?" Young yelped.

"Forget it," Curt said in deep disgust. "You two can't even go two minutes."

He stood and started to stalk to the mouth of the cave. Royal rushed after him and caught his arm. "I meant it, Curt. It's been mostly my fault. I'll keep my mouth shut. God, another thousand dollars would make this worthwhile."

Curt relented. "All right. I'll start now. I don't know when I'll be back."

"Take as long as you want," Royal said earnestly.

Curt thought about those two all the way to town. He might not be able to get any additional money from Jacob. If he didn't, the job was over. Either way, it would be a relief to get away from those bickering two.

It was only midafternoon when he rode into town. The bank should be open. He was going straight to it. Jacob might strenuously object, but Curt had reached the point where he no longer cared what Jacob objected to. Jacob might turn him down flat, thinking that Curt had already damaged the Kilmers enough. Somehow, Curt doubted that. Jacob had seemed so insatiable that the Kilmers be hurt that nothing would satisfy him. Curt wondered curiously about that driving need. Jacob had never told him what his purpose was.

Well, it didn't matter. All he wanted was to collect his money and get out of this cursed country.

He dismounted before the bank and walked inside. It must be a slack period, for there were no customers. He approached the bent man in the cage. "Will you tell Mr. Keeley it is imperative that I see him?"

"Who shall I tell him wants to see him?"

Curt shook his head. "Just tell him it's important. I won't leave until I see him."

"I'll tell him," the old man said. "I don't know how he'll react."

"You just try," Curt said in a hard voice.

The old man looked back at him a half-dozen times as he crossed to the door at the end of the room. Doubt was written all over his face. Curt almost laughed aloud. What would the old man think if he knew his real purpose for being here?

"What is it, Benson?" Keeley asked irritably. He had told the old fool that he was too busy to be disturbed today, and here was Benson insisting.

"There's a man outside who demands to see you," Benson said. He couldn't keep his voice from trembling. He wished this disturbing incident wouldn't be happening. He was too old to handle it.

"Go back and get his name," Keeley said sharply. "If he still refuses to give it, show him out."

Now the trembling extended all over Benson's body. It wasn't that he felt any physical danger in the man, but the whole thing was out of the ordinary.

He was gone for only a few seconds, then he came back and said, "He says his name is Curt. He wouldn't give his last name."

Keeley felt as though he had been kicked in the stomach. He had insisted that Curt never appear here, yet he was waiting outside his office. For a moment he felt as though his heart had stopped. He managed to draw a shaky breath and said in a reasonably normal tone, "Show him in." His voice sharpened. "Move, you old fool. How many times do I have to tell you?"

Benson came back with Curt in tow. Keeley didn't say anything, but he was livid.

"Hello, Jacob," Curt said. Was that a mocking in his voice? Benson didn't know.

"That's all, Benson. Get back to your work." Keeley waited until the door closed behind Benson, then moved to it, opened it, and peeked outside. He reclosed the door, and it was surprising that with so much anger in him he could control his voice.

"I told you never to come here. What the hell do you think you're doing?"

It didn't bother Curt. He sank into a chair. "I had to talk to you, Jacob. Have you heard what's happened?"

"You mean about the Kilmer sheep. There's some talk about it in town. Raines is a raving madman. You're risking a lot coming here."

Curt was untouched. "That's what I want to talk to you about. Do you consider the job finished?"

Keeley's brow knit as he thought for a moment. "It could possibly do the job. But to make certain, destroy another flock. Then I'm sure the Kilmers can't make a payment of any kind."

"Have you any suggestions of how I do that job?" The jeering was almost apparent in Curt's voice.

"A fast, quick way would be to use dynamite. You wouldn't have to get very close to use it. If it's handled properly, you could be gone almost before it blows up."

"You surprise me." The jeering was still in Curt's voice. "For a bank president to know so much about dynamite."

Keeley's face fell. "Are you saying you won't use it? Are you afraid to?"

"They taught me to use dynamite in prison, Jacob. That isn't the big problem."

Keeley frowned at his brother. "What *is* the problem, then?"

"Money! You didn't give me enough to finish the job as you want it. It'll take another five thousand dollars." Curt smiled. "A little trouble with my labor force. They won't work without more money."

Keeley paled, and he made little choking sounds. "That's a plain holdup," he squalled.

"Don't give me that injured look," Curt said. "I told you before it's costing me a heap of money. Now it seems I've got to buy dynamite. I've got a hunch you'll come out of this with a lot more than you're paying me. But it's all right with me if you don't want to pay what the job's worth. We'll call it quits with no hard feelings." He stood and started toward the door.

Keeley drummed on his desk with his fingertips, and the tempo showed how agitated he was. Oh God! He was so close to success, and here this stiff-necked brother promised to ruin everything. He suddenly caved in. "When do you want the money?" he whimpered.

"Right now. Before I leave. Save me a trip of coming back. You'd rest a lot easier knowing the job will be completed." His smile grew more brittle.

Keeley managed to choke off a sob. "I'll go get it," he mumbled.

He thought of what he had to tell Benson. All he could think of was that he was making a loan. Benson was in no position to question him about anything.

He walked into the vault and counted out five thousand dollars. His hands felt clammy and wet. He had to tell Benson something to keep his suspicions from rising.

He came out of the vault and said, "Benson, I've just taken five thousand dollars from the vault. I'm going back to my office to make out the loan papers."

He didn't like the questions rising in Benson's eyes, but Benson didn't dare voice them. "Give me a loan form."

"Yes, sir," Benson said.

Keeley returned to his office and sat down at his desk.

"Something bad happen out there?" Curt asked. "You look pale as a ghost."

"Nothing that bad," Keeley mumbled. He pulled the money out of his pocket and shoved it across the desk. "Count it."

Curt's teeth flashed. "I trust you." He stuffed the money in his pocket without counting it. "What's that for?" he asked curiously as Keeley began writing on a form.

"I've got to fill out a loan form to cover that five thousand dollars," he said angrily.

Curt chuckled. "I hope the name you pick out is a thoroughly reliable man." He adjusted his hat to a jaunty angle. "You can count the job done, Jacob. I probably won't see you again."

Keeley wanted to say, I hope not, but he kept his lips clamped. All he wanted to hear was that Curt had left the country for good. He scowlingly went back to filling out the loan form. This was clerk work. Benson should be doing it. But this should keep a lid on Benson's curiosity.

CHAPTER 18

Curt lugged his saddle into the cave. Royal and Young were at the far end. So far, Curt hadn't heard sounds of argument between them.

"How'd you come out?" Royal asked. He couldn't keep the eagerness out of his voice.

Young didn't say anything. His eyes just begged.

Curt pulled two thousand dollars out of his pocket. On the way here, he had separated the original five thousand dollars. Three of the sum was in his other pocket. "I told you I'd get it," he said with composure.

Young's hands shook as his fingers closed on his share. He looked like he was going to cry. Curt couldn't blame him. Two thousand dollars would carry him a long way.

Royal kept running the bills through his fingers. Curt didn't see any gratitude in his face. In fact, he looked suspicious. "Where's *your* share?" Royal demanded.

"In my pocket," Curt replied, his voice hardening. He had made a mistake. He should have kept three thousand dollars together and let them see him divide it up. "Is something wrong with that?" he asked sharply.

"Maybe not," Royal replied. "And maybe yes. I'm just wondering how much money you got originally. Maybe it was more than three thousand."

Curt tried to look injured. "You sound like you don't trust me."

"You could be right," Royal said, nodding slowly.

Curt had to get the subject changed as quickly as possible. "There's a little more to be done. The boss wants another Kilmer flock destroyed."

"It might not be a good idea," Royal said skeptically. "After all the hell we've raised, they'll be watching closer this time."

"We'll do it differently," Curt said easily. "I bought some dynamite while I was in town. We won't have to get as close. A couple of sticks tossed into a corral"—he raised his hands in a sharp upward thrust—"and there goes your flock."

Royal didn't look as sure. "I never handled any dynamite. It's damned dangerous stuff."

"Quit worrying," Curt snapped. "I learned how to handle it in prison. I'll take care of everything."

Up to now, Young hadn't said a word. "Does this mean you're planning on leaving me alone again?"

Curt flushed with anger, and Royal said, "Why, we wouldn't do that, Young. We're taking you with us."

Young missed that Royal was joshing him. "But I can't go," he objected. "This ankle won't let me ride, let alone walk."

"Why, I never thought of that," Royal said in pretended amazement.

They were ready to go at it again, and Curt said wearily, "Hold it, you two. Young, use your head. You didn't get that extra money for nothing. We've got to finish the job. We won't be gone more than a day, no more than two at the most. I'll cut you some firewood and stack it where it's handy."

The sullenness was growing deeper on Young's face, and Curt lost the last of his patience. "Damn it, Young. You've done nothing to earn your money. It seems you could keep your mouth shut."

"Not him," Royal said sarcastically. "It's easier for him to complain."

"That's right," Young screamed. "Both of you get on me. I wish to God I'd never come in with you."

"You know something, Young," Curt said evenly. "That makes two of us." He picked up the ax and started out of the cave. "Want to give me a hand with this, Royal?"

"I don't see why I should," Royal replied in a surly tone. "He can starve or freeze to death as far as I'm concerned. Oh hell." He got to his feet and followed Curt outside.

Curt picked out a dead tree and chopped vigorously to work off some of his anger. "Of all the ungrateful—" He broke off and grinned sheepishly at Royal. "Didn't some smart man once say you don't know a man until you live with him awhile?"

"Let me have that ax," Royal said. "I dunno. If he did, I didn't hear about it. But it sure fits Young. I'll be damned glad when I see the last of him."

"Two of us, Royal."

They worked a good hour, getting the tree down and chopped up into usable lengths. Then it took time to carry the wood into the cave.

"We'll be leaving now, Young," Curt tried to say pleasantly. "You've got plenty of food and firewood. Just keep off that ankle and let it rest. I'll bet when we get back it'll be almost healed."

"A hell of a lot you care," Young replied. He refused to meet Curt's eyes.

"Why, you little ingrate—" Royal started.

Curt caught his arm, stopping him. "You're not going to get through to him, Royal. Let's get this over."

He picked up his saddle and didn't look back at the cave until he was some forty yards from the entrance. "I hope he has enough sense to stay inside," he said, worry showing in his voice. "Nobody will see him if he's careful."

Royal shook his head. "I'm not sure he has enough sense to do that. Oh God, Curt. I'll be glad when this is over."

"Two of us," Curt said fervently.

CHAPTER 19

Curt and Royal had thoroughly checked out the Kilmer land. They moved with extreme caution. They never knew when an irritated owner would charge down on them, or simply blast them before their attacker could be seen. They located all the sheep flocks. With a clear sense of the lay of the land, they could pick out the point of their next attack.

They picked the hut furthest from the house. It was a good ten miles away. Even if the landowner learned immediately about their attack, it would take him time to get here.

They had crawled up to the crest of a hill and lay on their bellies, watching the hut and its flimsy corral.

"What do you think, Royal?"

"About as good as we can pick out," Royal answered. They had watched the herder move his flock out in the morning. "What do we do, wait until he returns tonight?"

"I don't see any other course," Curt grunted. He stretched out comfortably and cushioned his head in his locked hands. "Maybe we'll get lucky. If the herder takes the dog into his hut to feed him, maybe we won't have to shoot either of them."

"You getting squeamish?" Royal jeered.

"Not that," Curt answered seriously. "But we've run up a sizable score. If they ever catch up with us—" He let the words trail away.

"You think too much," Royal said mockingly.

"Maybe," Curt returned. "But if it's possible, I'd like to see what's ahead of me."

It seemed like an unusually long day. Outside of shifting their positions, there was nothing else to do.

A whiskey jay lit in a nearby tree and inspected them with those beady little eyes. He decided he didn't like what he saw, for he broke out in raucous protest.

He kept it up until it grated on Curt's nerves. He searched about him until he found a fair-sized pebble. He sat up to make his toss.

He didn't hit the jay, but he scared him, for the bird flew off with a frenzied beating of his wings. His shrill complaining carried back to them.

"Do you think that was wise, Curt, chasing him away like that?"

"It was wiser than to let him sit up there and announce to anybody that might pass this way that something was bothering him. At least I moved him."

"I think both of us have got tight nerves, Curt."

Curt managed a strained grin. "You could be right, Royal."

Neither man had spent a longer day. Curt could swear that not a single minute had passed, but he could look at the shadows of the sun and see where he was wrong. They were lengthening in the afternoon, and that told him time was passing, even if slowly.

Royal started to say something, and Curt reached over and pressed his arm. "Do you hear something, Royal?"

Royal shook his head. "I guess your ears are better than mine. Ah," he said in relieved satisfaction. "That's sheep coming."

It certainly was. The bleating grew louder, and Curt and Royal flattened against the ground.

Curt lifted his head for a brief peek. The corral was open, and the herder and the dog were busy driving the sheep into it. In that brief glimpse, Curt had to admire the dexterity of the dog. He not only had speed, he had cunning that matched anything the sheep could put out. He anticipated a sheep's break before it actually happened, and a quick dash cut off the animal's attempt to run.

Slowly the sheep entered the corral, and the herder closed the gap and fastened the muslin in place. He bent down, patted the dog and walked toward the hut, the dog at his heels.

Curt saw him enter the hut, taking the dog with him. "He's going to feed the dog," he hissed. "Now it's our time to move."

He picked up the saddlebag containing the sticks of dynamite and went down the slope at a rapid walk. "Keep an eye on that door, Royal. If he opens it, you'll have to drop him." He hoped it wouldn't come to that. They had enough murders against their record.

They reached a spot not twenty yards from the corral. The sheep had noticed their presence, for they were beginning to race about the corral.

Curt dropped to his knees. "Get down, Royal," he hissed. "But keep your eye on that hut door." He capped a stick of dynamite and attached a short length of fuse. He set about immediately preparing a second stick.

"It's sure taking you plenty of time," Royal groused.

"I'm getting two sticks ready," Curt explained. "Get down against the ground." He rose to his knees, touched a match to the fuse, watched its spluttering, then drew back his arm.

His toss was good. It landed in the middle of the corral. His experience with dynamite had taught him that most of the force of the explosion went upwards. Even at this relatively short distance they were safe here.

His ears heard the blast of the explosion, and his body felt the vibrations running through the earth. He immediately rose to his knees. He glanced at the hut door, and it remained closed. Either the herder hadn't had time to react to the first explosion, or he was wise enough not to explore the cause.

Curt fired the second fuse, made his toss, and flattened himself against the ground. It seemed an agonizingly long time before the second explosion. The first one hadn't got all the sheep, for he could hear some of them crying in their fright. The second explosion should erase all sound from the corral. It seemed forever before the second explosion came, and Curt knew that was only a figment of his imagination. Both lengths of the fuse burned at the same rate.

The explosion came with the same ear-shattering roar. Curt rose and glanced at the hut door. It was still closed. "Let's get out of here, Royal."

They crabbed backward as fast as they could go. After a hundred yards, Curt thought it was safe to rise. They scrambled to their feet and ran, crouched low. At any second, Curt half-expected to hear the sharp crack of a rifle. It didn't come. He had completed their third attack with no retaliation. He guessed Royal was right when he said their nerves were beginning to bite them. Curt knew they'd better get off Kilmer land as fast as they could make it.

CHAPTER 20

Miller gripped his rifle with an intensity that made his hands ache. He had heard the two explosions coming in quick succession, but he hadn't been foolish enough to investigate. He knew with an innate wisdom that if he stepped outside this hut he would be cut down. It had happened to Mendoza.

The dog whimpered uneasily at his side, and Miller reached over to pet it. "Scared, boy?" he asked in a low voice. "That makes two of us. We'll just stay inside here until we're absolutely sure that whoever's out there is gone."

He didn't have a watch or a clock, for time had never meant anything to him. But he was absolutely positive that an hour had passed. It had to have; he had never packed so much waiting in a period of time.

Though he felt positive, he still waited a little longer. He grinned weakly and shook his head. He couldn't spend the rest of his life cowering in here.

He made sure a shell was in the rifle's chamber, and holding the rifle ready in one hand, he opened the door. The tension gripped him, making his guts ache. The dog had no such qualms. It dashed outside, barking madly. The tension increased for Miller. Was somebody still out there?

He sucked in a deep breath to fortify himself before he took that first tentative step. Nothing happened to disturb the eerie quiet. But he did notice a strange, pungent smell. The smell seemed to hover stronger over the corral, and Miller puzzled over it. That had to be connected with the explosions. Then Miller had it. That smell was the aftermath of dynamite, and he was certain of what he would find.

The night was dark, for the moon wasn't up yet. Miller took hesitant, trembling steps toward the corral. Another smell permeated the first pungent smell, and he identified that instantly. That was blood and mangled flesh.

The dog had quit barking. He came back to Miller and cringed, whimpering against his leg. "I think the danger is all over, Captain," Miller said, patting the dog's head.

He couldn't make out details too plainly until he was right up against the corral, or rather where the corral had been. Some great force had torn the muslin into tatters, and pieces of it littered the ground like a light snowfall. Masses of mangled animal bodies were piled up everywhere he looked. He retched at the horrible sight, and for a moment was certain his stomach would empty. He turned and stumbled blindly back toward the wagon. There was nothing he or anybody else could do for those poor, hapless sheep.

The horse that pulled the wagon was staked out some hundred yards from the wagon, and Miller's fingers shook so badly he didn't think he could get the animal harnessed. He finally made it, called the dog up onto the seat beside him, then turned the horse toward the Kilmer house. He drove as recklessly as he could on a dark night. He had a terrible report to bring to Jessie. He reworded it a dozen times in his mind. There would be no easy way of relating what had happened.

He pulled up before the house and jumped down, yelling at the top of his lungs, "Jessie, Jessie."

It seemed forever before he got any response, and impatience was literally shaking him to pieces. My God, he had yelled loud enough to wake the dead. A light finally appeared in the kitchen window, and Miller ran to the door and pounded on it. He didn't realize his urgency was making him babble. He couldn't have told anybody what he was saying.

The door opened, and Jessie in his nightshirt stood there. "What the hell?" he started, then his eyes rounded as he saw who was there. "Miller!" he exclaimed. "What are you doing here? You should be out with your flock."

"There ain't no flock," Miller cried. His lips trembled so hard they garbled his words. "They were all blown to hell."

Jessie reached out a hand to steady him, then led him to a chair, and pressed him down into it. He crossed quickly to a cupboard, opened it, and pulled out a bottle of whiskey. He poured out a stiff drink and handed it to Miller. "Drink this, Carl. It'll help steady you down."

The first swallow choked Miller, and he gasped while his eyes ran water. It took three more swallows to empty his glass.

The tapping of Asa's cane could be heard coming toward the

kitchen. The door opened, and Asa was there, his eyes bleary from interrupted sleep.

"What the hell's going on here?" he asked petulantly.

"Carl came in with a story about an explosion. Start it over, Carl. Asa wants to hear it too."

Miller told his story evenly enough, though he choked every now and then. "I didn't go out after those two explosions." He looked pleadingly at the two stern faces. He didn't want them blaming him. "I remembered what happened to Mendoza," he said. "I sure didn't want to step out into a hail of bullets."

"You did right," Jessie approved. "How long did you stay in the hut?"

"It seemed like forever. I know it was better than an hour," Miller replied. "I smelled this acrid odor the minute I stepped outside. I never been around dynamite, but from what I've heard about it, that explosion and smell could have come from what was described to me."

"Go on," Jessie said, his lips compressed.

"I hurried down to where the corral was." Miller briefly closed his eyes as though he was trying to shut out a scene forever etched on his mind. "All I found was sheep blown to hell. I didn't see any movement. If any of them were alive, I missed them. The muslin was blown all to hell. If any sheep were alive, they'd escaped."

Jessie smashed a fist into a palm. "That's dynamite, all right. And I know who did it."

Asa looked anxiously at him. "Who was it, Jessie?"

"The goddamned Hagens. Don't tell me I'm wrong. Didn't they use dynamite last year when they blasted a new opening to Kirby Creek? They wanted to divert it so they could water that piece of low ground."

"You're going to tell Raines of your suspicions first, Jessie?" Asa begged.

"I am not," Jessie snapped. "He's had two chances to arrest them. He didn't do a damned thing either time. This time I'll take care of it myself."

"Oh God," Asa said, perturbed. "You know what that means."

"I know," Jessie said wildly. "It means we're broke. There's no possible way of meeting that payment. Tell him again? Hell, no. Carl, you can tell him about those mangled sheep. Maybe that'll change Raines's mind."

"Jessie, how do you figure going about it?"

"I'm taking every man available. First, I want to look at those destroyed sheep. Then I'm heading straight for the Hagens'."

Asa sighed. "I wish to God I knew whether or not you're right. If you blunder, you've blown off the lid of hell."

Jessie bristled at the quiet censure behind Asa's words. "I know I'm right," he snapped. "I'll stand behind anything I do."

"You'll have to," Asa said mournfully. He waited until Jessie was dressed, then said, "All the good luck in the world, boy."

"Sure," Jessie said gruffly. He wanted to go over to his grandfather, hug him, and tell him everything was going to be all right. Some restraint was between them, and that aroused his resentment even more. He wasn't used to restraint between Asa and himself.

He aroused four men, and Miller said, "I'm going too, Jessie."

Jessie looked doubtfully at him. "It could be pretty messy, Carl. The Hagens keep quite a few riders around."

"Those were *my* sheep," Miller said fiercely.

Jessie reached out and squeezed his shoulder. "You've got every right," he agreed.

Just recounting what had happened erased the sleepy look from all faces. It wasn't as grim as it would be when they looked at the scene of destruction, Jessie thought.

He fretted while they saddled. When a man was driven, every delay seemed inordinately long. He didn't know what he was leading these men into. He could only be certain of one thing; it wouldn't be good.

It was a silent ride to where Miller's wagon had been. Jessie didn't know what he could say to lighten their mood, and even if he knew, he didn't want to.

Miller rode beside Jessie. "Right up ahead," he muttered.

Jessie nodded. He knew the location. He held up a hand as a sound drifted to him and halted the small cavalcade. "Sounds like animals fighting," one of the men said in a low voice.

Jessie knew what it was. That was the noise of predators fighting over the easy spoils. He caught a shady glimpse of them as the horses moved forward. He saw wolves and coyotes. The coyotes dodged the savage slash of teeth when the lesser animals encroached upon the wolves' territory.

Several of the men threw up rifles. Jessie started to stop them, then reconsidered. Killing a few predators would probably be the only favorable thing to be gained tonight. He had grown up with an inborn hatred of wolves and coyotes. Even if some of them weren't dropped, the gunfire would drive them away.

"Cut them down," he said in a choked voice. A sheepman worked so damned hard, then these four-legged scavengers wrested his rewards from him. Added to that list was the two-legged kind, the more deadly kind, for in a night or two they could wipe out the effort of years.

The predators were so absorbed in their grisly picnic that the horsemen were able to get fairly close to them.

Jessie fired the first shot, and he dropped a wolf. A fusillade of shots rang out, and more of the scavengers fell. Some of them were only wounded, for they snapped and clawed at the stinging hurts that suddenly developed. In an instant, all of them were going, slinking away into the night.

Some of Jessie's men wanted to go after them, and Jessie wearily shook his head. It wouldn't do any good. He rode up to the remains of what was once a flock of sheep. His stomach rose and fell back into its ordinary place. The carnage made a man want to vomit.

"I want the Hagens," he said. "Let's get riding."

CHAPTER 21

They were on Hagen land now, and Jessie raised a hand, slowing down the headlong rush. He didn't know what they were riding into.

"Let's see what's ahead of us," he said grimly. He frowned as he looked at the red that had suddenly risen into the sky ahead of them.

"What's that?" Miller asked in a taut voice.

Jessie shook his head. He hadn't the slightest idea. The only thing he could think of was fire. It had to be a sizable one to so enlighten the sky.

They cautiously rode out into the clearing around the Hagen house, and Jessie choked back a cry. He didn't know what had caused the fire, but one side of the house was completely enveloped. With a fire of this magnitude, Jessie was surprised he saw no figures rushing about, trying to control the flames. Maybe the Hagens weren't at home.

He stopped his horse and started to dismount. "You don't intend to go in there," Miller said in an awed voice.

"I've got to," Jessie said simply. Fire was the most dreaded thing of all, particularly when it struck at night. Man was so helpless against it.

"No," Miller said stubbornly.

"There might be some people trapped in that house," Jessie said. He dropped to the ground. With each step toward the house, the heat grew more intense. It was a chilly night, and away from the heat a man needed a sheepskin. Jessie slipped out of his and dropped it on the ground. He wouldn't need it anymore from here on.

He looked back, and men were following him. If Jessie could go into this inferno, they could too.

Jessie shielded his face with an arm and darted through the front door. The interior of the house was filled with smoke, but the flames weren't as intense as they were in the back of the house.

Jessie and his men picked their way through the house, looking for trapped victims. This was a clapboard house, and with the breeze stirring the flames, it wouldn't last long. He started to go into a room and hastily reclosed the door. The flames were in full stride in this room. Jessie caught a glimpse of a wood-burning stove and guessed what had happened. The stove door was open, and the metal carpet beneath the stove was too small. Somebody had risen during the night and restocked the stove, then forgot to close the door. A piece of burning wood had popped out of the stove with such velocity that it missed the metal entirely. It had laid on the bare floor and smoldered until the flooring heated up and caught fire. Without somebody around to keep an alert eye on it, the fire had spread. Jessie had no idea how much time it would take to have the entire house burning, but however much, the time was enough.

"Look in every room you can reach," he said, his voice tight. He headed for a door straight ahead of him. Just before he reached it, it opened and Grat staggered out. He was choking, and his eyes were reddened. "God Almighty," Grat said. "What's happening?"

"Your house is on fire," Jessie said. "You'd better get out as quick as you can."

He reached for Grat's arm, and Grat threw aside his hand. "Gary's in there," he panted. "He's too drunk to even be aroused."

"Take Grat out," Jessie ordered two of his men. He headed straight for the door Grat had just come out. It too was beginning to fill with smoke, and the air was noticeably hotter.

He spent a few futile moments trying to arouse Gary, then bent over, got him into a sitting position and flung his weight over his shoulder.

He barely got out of the room when Miller and another man ran toward him. "We'll take him, Jessie," Miller said. "Grat said his father is still in the house."

"I'll check," Jessie said tersely. It might have been his imagination, but the temperature in the house seemed to have risen, and there was a swaying in the roof timbers. An ominous crackling filled the air. The house was going at any moment. He wished he knew which was Wirt's room. He was afraid he didn't have much time.

He looked in one room, and it was empty. A sense of urgency was beginning to drive him. Maybe it was premonition, but he couldn't stay in this house much longer.

He looked in the next room, and Wirt lay on his back, his mouth open, deep snores coming from it.

Jessie didn't waste time trying to awaken him. Wirt was a slight man, and the sense of urgency said, Pick him up. And hurry.

Jessie slung him over his shoulder. His eyes were running water, and the smoke had thickened. For a moment, he was afraid his senses were becoming confused, for he couldn't remember which way the front door lay.

"Here now," he mumbled, trying to get a grip on his slipping senses. "None of that now."

He turned and walked directly to the front door. Thank God, it had been left open. He didn't have to fight Wirt's weight while he fumbled for the doorknob. The crackling overhead grew more ominous, and he wanted to break into a run. That wouldn't do, either, for his haste might cause him to trip. He kept his head down, planting each foot firmly and steadily. He kept his head pulled in as tightly as he could get it to his chest. It probably didn't help any, but he thought it did.

He could tell when he was outside by the cooling of the air. He must be a fair distance from the burning house, and he wanted to look at it. No, he counseled himself. His big job right now was getting Wirt to a place he absolutely knew was safe.

Somebody was trying to take Wirt off his shoulder, and Jessie momentarily resisted those hands.

"It's all right, Jessie," a gruff voice said. "It's Grat. I'll take him."

Jessie gladly let go of that awkward weight. Now his legs could tremble, and they shook so they refused to support him.

"Over here, Jessie," Grat called. He had Wirt laid out beside Gary, and he patted the ground beside them. "Man, you look done in."

"As close as I ever want to be," Jessie confessed. He sank to the ground and indulged in the luxury of filling his lungs with cool, clean air. His face smarted, and he wondered if he was burned. He touched fingers to a cheek and decided he wasn't. The flesh was still firm and not puffy.

"There it goes," Grat said suddenly.

His words jerked Jessie's head toward the burning house. The house was going. The fire had weakened the timber, and Jessie could actually see the swaying of the structure. The house went all at once. The strain on the timbers made them groan, giving the house an almost human sound. The house collapsed, the flames momentarily leaping high, spewing out a towering stream of sparks. Then the flames suddenly lowered, and the sparks died out.

"Goddamn it," Grat said. There was no rage in his tone, only a profound sorrow. Jessie could understand that. When a man watched his house burn, it ripped something out of him.

Grat swung his head toward Jessie. "It can be rebuilt," he said gruffly. "You got us out just in time. I don't think you had a minute left."

"I did what I had to do," Jessie said stiffly. The resentment was flowing back in. He had come here to even up scores with the Hagens, and here he had ended up by saving their lives.

Gary had come to and was sitting up, staring foolishly about him. Wirt was still stretched out on the ground.

"Wirt all right?" Jessie managed to ask above his resentment. How did a man react to others he had sworn to kill just a short while ago.

Grat looked at his father. "He's all right. Just drunk. That's all. The older Pa gets, the poorer drinker he is. It doesn't take much to put him out." His voice sobered. "I'm glad he didn't see this. Pa built that house."

It was unbelievable how a near tragedy changed the trend of a man's emotions. There was no hostility in Grat at all. "Jessie, I don't know how to put this." He struggled with his words for a moment. "You saved our lives."

"I didn't come here for that," Jessie said flatly. "I came here to kill you."

Grat was so big-eyed that he looked ludicrous. "What the hell—" He changed his words. "Why did you change?"

"I couldn't stand by and let you burn to death," Jessie said.

"Did you hate us that much, Jessie?"

"I did when I looked at my flock of sheep. They were blown all to hell. The wolves and coyotes were fighting over the remains."

Comprehension flooded Grat's eyes. "You thought *we* did that?"

"It crossed my mind," Jessie said simply.

"Oh, good Lord," Grat said. That came as close to a prayer as he would ever make. "I swear to God, Jessie, we didn't have anything to do with it. We'd made a big shipment of cattle today. We started drinking in town and brought some bottles back here with us. We got roaring drunk. We took the house, and the riders went to the bunkhouse." He looked at the building, and disgust was in his voice. "Shows how drunk everybody got. The riders haven't even shown up yet. Ah," he said, his voice flat. "Here comes a few of them now."

He drew a deep breath. "I remember carrying Pa to bed. The last thing I recall was telling Gary to chunk a few logs in the fire. It was getting chilly. Do you suppose that fire started from that?"

"I'm afraid it did, Grat. I caught a glimpse of that stove. The door was open. I think a spark missed the metal rug and landed on the bare floor. I don't know how long it took, but it got a start."

Grat stared at him with awed eyes. "That goddamned Gary. I'll chew his butt out good—" He stopped and shook his head. "It doesn't matter now. We got out alive, thanks to you. I been telling Pa the last couple of years we had to get a bigger metal carpet. Twice I saw sparks fly out and smolder against the wooden floor. Both times I was there and sober. It was no trick to stamp them out. This time I wasn't sober or even around." His head sank into his hands, and he was lost in his thoughts. "You really believe we blew up your sheep?"

"I was damned positive of it," Jessie said firmly. "It's a good thing we didn't find you when we first rode up. The sight of the house on fire drove all other thoughts out of our heads."

There was a tremor in Grat's voice. "I swear to you, Jessie, we didn't have anything to do with it."

"I believe you now," Jessie said soberly. "I wouldn't have listened to you before. Isn't it funny how things develop? I was so positive you were involved that I didn't wait to talk to Raines. I thought he was on your side. Twice before he cleared you. I wasn't going to let that happen again." He grinned wanly. "And here we're talking sanely to each other."

Grat reached out a hand, and Jessie took it without hesitation. "Jessie, I swear to you we had nothing to do with your trouble. I couldn't have said that in the past. We wanted to do anything that would hurt you, though we didn't have anything to do with your father's death. A Kimberly hand was responsible for that. He got out of the country as fast as he could go. I knew about it, but I kept my mouth shut. You know how things were." He shrugged and emotion moved his face. "Things changed. After that judge lectured us, I made damned sure we never even thought of lifting a finger at you."

"Somebody didn't feel that way," Jessie said dully. "Grat, did any of the other cattlemen mention something that might lead you to think they were trying to stir up the old trouble?"

The expression on Grat's face showed how seriously he considered Jessie's question. "If one of them is behind this, Jessie, I never heard about it. I don't think any of them had any such ideas. If I knew, or even had a suggestion, I'd tell you."

Jessie grunted. He believed Grat. Tonight's happening was enough to make any man stick to the truth. "Well, somebody is behind this," he said wearily. "It doesn't matter now," he said, defeat heavy in his voice. "The Kilmers are done for. We can't make it through the year after all the losses we've had."

Grat started to answer, and three of his riders came up to him. "My God, Grat," one of them cried. "What happened?"

"You've got eyes, haven't you? We had a fire."

"Jesus," the man gasped. "Was anybody hurt?"

"Thanks to Jessie, there wasn't. He came up and pulled us out." The man looked owl-eyed at Jessie. "You mean Jessie Kilmer?"

"Oh, damn it," Grat said in exasperation. "You're looking straight at him."

"But I thought—" the man stammered.

"That's past thinking," Grat snapped. "From now on, Jessie Kilmer is the best friend the Hagens will ever have."

He looked at Jessie, his eyes shining with a new thought. "Jessie, something just occurred to me. Starting at daylight, every rider the Hagens have plus your men will set out to find out who might be behind all your trouble." Jessie started to object, and Grat held up a hand. "Don't you let a man pay back some of what he owes?"

Jessie grinned wanly. "That was all I could do. But there's so many things in the way of what you say. We need breakfast, and you're sure in no position to feed anybody now."

Grat chuckled. "You think so? The bunkhouse has a small cook-stove. We keep coffee and cups there. The boys can get a cup of coffee anytime they want it. There's a supply of jerky down there. Keeps hunger pangs from working on the boys. It won't be fancy, but it'll fill you up."

"That'll do just fine," Jessie acknowledged. He called Miller over. "Carl, go back to the house and tell Asa I won't be home for a day or two." He hesitated a moment, then said, "Tell him what's happened here. He's got a right to know what's going on."

Miller looked disappointed. "I'd have liked to be in on the windup if you do find anybody."

"This is just as important," Jessie assured him.

He watched Miller mount and ride away, then turned to Grat. "Grat, I sure could use some of that coffee now."

"I think I could too." He walked over and prodded Wirt with a boot toe. "Come on, you old coot. Wake up."

Wirt was beginning to come to, for he was stirring and muttering incoherently. "Gary," Grat ordered. "Stay with him until he fully comes to. Then bring him down to the bunkhouse."

He shook his head as he walked away with Jessie. "He'll turn the air blue when he comes to and realizes what's happened."

"I feel sorry for him," Jessie said sympathetically. "Hell of a blow when a man learns he's lost his house."

"How right you are." Grat shook his head. "It's tearing my guts apart when I think of some of the things I lost in that fire." He shrugged. "Crying won't get them back. Want to go down to the bunkhouse and get that coffee?"

Jessie got his feet under him. Lord, he ached in every joint. "Sounds good to me, Grat." Funny how things worked out. He swore he'd never care for Grat Hagen, but he was learning that he wasn't so bad.

CHAPTER 22

"Not much of a breakfast, was it?" Grat asked as they walked out to their horses. Jessie noticed that he glanced once at where the house had stood, then steadfastly didn't look that way again. Jessie grinned. "At least my belly isn't empty. It'll do. Where do we start, Grat?"

Grat scowled as he thought. He was taking every rider he had with him, leaving only Gary to look after Wirt. With the four Jessie had, it made quite a force.

"I figure somebody's doing some hiding out," Grat said reflectively. "Still, it seems like strangers would have been seen. But nobody's reported a glimpse of them."

Two people probably saw them, Jessie thought soberly. His two dead herders might have caught a glimpse of them. If they had, nobody would ever know about it.

"Do you know Tillery's land?" Grat asked.

Jessie nodded. He knew its location, but he had never been on it. He had made it certain that he never trespassed on a cattleman's land.

"Most of that place is rough land," Grat went on. "Trees and mountains. So rough that it's little use for grazing." He narrowed his eyes. "If I wanted to hide out, I'd certainly go there. That's probably why none of Tillery's help have seen anybody."

Jessie's heart sank at Grat's description of the land. It was going to be difficult, if not impossible, to find a few men on a place that rough.

Grat caught the uncertainty on Jessie's face and said, "It's a place to start looking, isn't it?"

"Tillery's land," Grat announced as they entered a scraggly brush-covered land. The sun was up full, and Jessie could feel the sweat start to pop out on him.

Grat chuckled at the look on Jessie's face. "It gets worse. Spread out," he called to the men behind him. "Stay within calling distance. If you find something interesting, sing out."

Jessie doubted that anybody would find anything. Maybe he was in a depressed mood this morning. It wouldn't do much good if they did find out who was behind all this trouble. His sheep business was gone. The payment was coming up fast, and there was no way now he could meet it.

Jessie cocked an eye at the sky. It must be getting close to noon, and they hadn't uncovered anything yet. The land grew rougher, the brush had thickened into trees. Grat was right when he said this was damned poor grazing ground.

"Grat, over here," a voice called from Jessie's left.

Grat pointed in the direction of the call, and Jessie's eyes caught a gleam in Grat's eyes. Maybe something was happening.

"Keep calling," Grat yelled back. They needed the sound of that voice to guide them.

"It's Sam," Grat said, as the form of a horseman materialized in the brush and timber. "You got something, Sam?" he asked as he urged his horse up to him.

"Just that," Sam said, jerking a thumb at a horse tied in the timber. "Damned odd place to find a horse."

"Do you know him?" Grat asked, studying the nondescript bay.

Sam shook his head. "To the best of my knowledge, I never saw him before."

"Sam knows about every horse in this county," Grat remarked. He and Jessie and Sam dismounted for a closer study of the animal. They viewed it from all angles, and Sam came up with a possible solution. "I don't know the brand. Some of the horse traders keep bringing in strange horses. This could be one of them."

Grat nodded solemnly. "Look at the way he's tied. Somebody plans on using him." He pointed at the horse droppings behind the animal. "He's eaten fairly recently. I'd guess the owner is nearby. If not, we'll wait him out and see if he returns."

Jessie could feel the accelerated beat of his heart. They were near to something; he could feel it. "Shall we look around a little more? We can always come back here."

"Good idea," Grat approved. "This grove is pretty thick. It might explain why somebody is using it. They don't want to be seen."

Jessie's fingernails bit into his palm. Oh God, how he would like to run across the culprit behind the destruction of his sheep.

They spread out and came out of the thicker timber. They made a long, extended line. Jessie didn't know what they were looking for; he only hoped they would find something.

"Grat," he said in a low voice. "Up ahead. Somebody's cut down a dead tree. Limbs all over. Ah," he said with immense satisfaction as they neared the spot. "They did quite a bit of chopping. Chips everywhere."

"They picked a dead tree," Grat said speculatively. "Somebody wanted wood for a fire. As much trouble as they went to not to be seen, I'd say they picked a fairly obscure spot. Now, where would that be?" His eyes roamed over the bluff that rose ahead of them. "Jessie!" He gripped Jessie's arm, and his fingers bit deep. "Do you see that dark patch of shadow at the base of that cliff?"

Jessie had to search the bluff twice before he made out a dark shadow that didn't look quite natural. It could be an ideal hiding place. Brush grew up closely around it and blended well with the rock strata. "What do you think, Grat?" Jessie couldn't keep the quiver out of his voice.

"It could be a cave. If I was hiding out, I'd pick a spot like that," Grat answered. "We only stumbled across it by accident."

He drew a deep breath. "I've got a funny feeling, Jessie. What you've been looking for may be in that cave."

"I hope to God you're right," Jessie replied fervently.

Grat called the horsemen around him and issued orders. "Some of you take the horses and tie them out of sight. We don't know whether or not there's people in that cave."

He selected a half-dozen men to lead the horses away. He grinned tightly at Jessie and said, "Let's go in and check it out. Take it slow and easy. We may already have been spotted, and somebody is watching every step."

At the cave's mouth, he split the bunch into two groups. "We don't know what we're heading into," he warned. "Go in fast but be careful. Be ready to shoot at anything that moves."

He shifted his rifle into his right hand. He flashed another grin at Jessie and, bending low, darted inside.

Jessie was only a step behind him. He took the left side of the cave, Grat the right. Other men crowded in behind Grat and Jessie, and both men moved a little deeper into the cave to give them space.

After coming out of the brilliant sunshine, Jessie couldn't see anything but shadows inside the cave.

"Nobody here," he said, disappointment showing in his tone.

Grat had adjusted more quickly to the poorer light, for he said sharply, "Yes, there is. Huddled clear at the back of the cave."

Jessie's head lifted, and his eyes adjusted to the light. Something was back there, and he couldn't be positive whether or not that was a man's figure. "We'd better check it out," he said, tight-lipped.

They moved cautiously deeper into the cave, a tentative step at a time, both rifles ready. One wrong move, and both guns were ready to spit out lead.

"You back there," Grat said sharply. "You make a mistake, and you're a dead man."

The shadowy form emitted a startled squawk. "Don't shoot," it begged. "I ain't doing nothing."

"I guess we can be certain now, Jessie, that somebody's around," Grat said. All the tension was gone out of his voice.

They relaxed no caution as they moved on to the huddled figure. Either their eyes had adjusted better, or the light was stronger. The man sat crouched against a wall, his eyes furtive.

"Who are you?" Jessie demanded. "What are you doing here?"

"I ain't done nothing," the man whimpered. "You can't lay the blame on me."

Grat and Jessie exchanged suggestive glances. Both instinctively felt that the mystery would start unraveling now.

"I asked who you are," Jessie said more harshly.

"My name's Young." He tried to meet Jessie's eyes and couldn't.

"What are you doing here?" Jessie demanded again.

"I was just resting," Young whimpered. "I've got a bum ankle."

Jessie's eyes went to the bare foot. It was badly swollen. "That your horse tied out in that grove of trees?" Jessie asked. "How'd you get here after you tied it up?"

Young tried to grin. "I managed it, but believe me, it was tough."

Grat's patience ran out. He swung the rifle so that the muzzle bore directly at Young's face. "You know what I think, mister? I think you're a goddamned liar. You didn't tie that horse up, and you didn't do all that chopping out there. You didn't carry the firewood in, either. Who's in this with you, and what are you after?"

Young gulped to keep back a sob. He didn't know who these men were, but they knew everything about him and Curt and Royal.

Grat cocked the rifle, and it made a sharp, distinctive sound. "I'm not waiting much longer, mister. I'd just as soon shoot you as waste my time like this."

Young made a frightened bleat. He held out both hands in mute supplication. "I didn't have anything to do with this," he babbled. "I didn't want to go along with them, but they forced me."

"Who's 'they'?" Jessie asked, his eyes beginning to fire. He was

THE FEUD 157

only a step from knowing all the answers that had so battered him.

Grat threw the rifle butt to his shoulder and squinted down the barrel. "I'd tell him what he wants to know, mister," he said softly. "I'd say you got about ten seconds."

Young's eyes were frantic. "Curt and Royal," he stammered.

"Where are they now?"

Young shook his head. "I don't know."

"You expect them back?"

Young studied those two implacable faces. He licked his lips as he struggled to find the right words. The temptation to lie slowly faded from his mind.

"I think your best bet would be to tell the truth," Grat suggested. "It'll be damned easy to leave you here."

Young broke like a dish dropped on a hard surface. "I'll tell you whatever you want to know."

"Were you three involved in killing my sheep?" Jessie asked.

Young looked from face to face, and those savagely bright eyes impaled him. "I wasn't in on it," he cried. "I couldn't move around because of this bad ankle." He gestured at the foot stretched out before him. "I've been here all this time."

"But you knew what the other two were doing," Jessie said.

The pleading in Young's face faded as he looked at those relentless eyes. "I knew," he said weakly.

"You say they'll be back shortly?"

Young nodded. The weakness welled up inside him, and he wanted to cry. Curt and Royal would never forgive him for talking, but he had every right, didn't he? They'd gone away and left him while he was helpless.

"I expect them at any time." Young buried his face in his hands, and the muffled sound of his crying came distinctly.

"Jesus," Grat said in disgust. "A real bad one."

"The other two are probably mostly responsible," Jessie mused. "Do we wait in here for them to come back?"

Grat looked around the cave. "I can't think of a better place to wait." He walked to the mouth of the cave and called one of the men over to him.

"All of you see that the horses are well hid, and don't show yourselves. The big ones responsible for all the trouble should be back anytime. You keep out of sight until you see two men come in, then you can close any escape route." He glanced from face to face, his eyes hard. "Is that understood? I'll brain any man makes a move that warns them."

"There won't be any warning," one of them replied.

Grat reentered the cave. "Jessie, there's little niches in the cave walls. By pressing close into one, they won't see us. Why should they? They won't be expecting us."

He moved a few steps and stopped in front of Young. "I'm keeping this rifle trained on you. One squeal out of you, and I'll splatter your brains all over the floor."

Young's shaking was visible. "I won't say a word," he promised weakly.

"Just keep on being smart," Grat said. He took a gouged-out niche on the left-hand side of the cave. Jessie found a similar spot on the right-hand side. They had a plain view of the cave's entrance. A slight turn of the head brought Young into view. Now only the waiting remained.

CHAPTER 23

Curt uncinched his saddle and stripped it off. The saddle blanket dragged after it. He bent to retrieve both items.

"It took us long enough to get back here," Royal grumbled as he stripped the gear from his horse.

"You worried about Young?" Curt jeered.

"I haven't given him a thought," Royal said with brutal candor. "Though by now I'll bet he's crying all over the place. Why did you take so long getting back?" he asked curiously.

"I took the long way around," Curt answered, "for a good reason. After night before last, I'll bet part of the county is boiling. So we spent extra hours getting back. It was the safest way. One good thing happened, though," he said and grinned.

"What was that?" Royal asked, frowning.

"With all the time we took, the horses had ample opportunity to fill up. We won't have to think about that for quite a while."

Royal's frown didn't lessen. "It sounds like you're planning on remaining in that cave awhile longer."

"You figured right," Curt answered. "We'll stay put until we see how the county's reacting. When we finally leave, I want to believe the way will be clear." At Royal's groan, he asked, "That doesn't suit you?"

"I'm just thinking of spending more time around that bellyacher. I can't get out of this country quick enough." He shouldered his saddle and fell into step with Curt. "I should think you'd feel the same way."

"I do," Curt replied. "I want to get out of here just as fast as I can make it. I may have to stop in town to pick up a few personal things. I kept that hotel room."

Royal cocked a judging eye at him. "Like the money you made for this job."

"You'll never know, Royal," Curt answered and grinned.

They walked to the cave's entrance, and Curt looked all around.

"Nothing out of the ordinary, Royal. But do you know, I'm getting the oddest feeling, like somebody's watching us."

"You really got a case of nerves," Royal jeered. He raised his voice. "Hey, Young, we're back."

At Curt's surprised look, he said, "Just thought I'd let him know we're back. It'll give him time to get that complaining look off his face."

They stepped inside the cave, and Curt's eerie feeling grew stronger. He could almost swear that somebody else beside Young was in the cave.

He and Royal advanced toward the seated man. "Something bad happen, Young?" Curt asked. "You've got a funny look on your face."

"Hell, yes, something's happened," Royal said savagely. "Look at him. He's shaking all over."

All Young's restraint left him. "It's not my fault. They made me tell them."

Royal dropped his saddle and shifted his rifle into both hands. "What did you tell them, you bastard?"

"I told them what you've been doing," Young said, his voice cracking on every word. "I had to. They threatened to blow my head off."

"Why, you rotten little sneak," Royal said furiously. He swung the rifle into line with Young.

Grat stepped out of his niche. "Drop that gun, mister, or you're a dead man."

Royal's face was twisted into a fearsome mask. "The hell I will," he screamed. He already had a shell in the chamber and he squeezed the trigger. The impact of the bullet slammed Young against the cave wall. He hung there a moment, his face agonized. "I didn't want to tell—" His voice shattered, and he sprawled lifelessly on the ground.

Royal tried to swing and turn his rifle at the same time.

"You are a damned fool," Grat said. There was almost pity in his voice before he pulled the trigger. His bullet caught Royal before he completed his turn. It knocked Royal back several stumbling steps. He had the vitality of an ox, and he tried to hold on to his rifle while he fought for his balance.

"You learn the hard way," Grat said and pulled the trigger again. The second bullet plowed into Royal's chest, and his hand opened, releasing the rifle. He stared at Grat in stupefaction before he came all apart. He sprawled on the ground, his muscles and eyes going slack and lifeless.

It had happened so fast that Curt was slow to react to it. His face was stupefied, then resolution firmed it. "Why, damn you," he said and tried to raise his rifle.

"Don't try it," Jessie said in a frozen voice. "Drop it, unless you want to join Royal on the floor."

The judging of eyes held for a long moment. Jessie didn't want to have to kill him. He needed proof to take to Raines—who was behind all his trouble.

Curt's resolve broke, and he opened his hand, letting the rifle fall. He grinned weakly and said, "I guess I didn't want to die right now."

"You don't know how close you came to it," Jessie said gravely. "Why did you go after my sheep?"

Curt shrugged. "It wasn't my idea."

"Whose idea was it?"

Curt shook his head and didn't reply.

"You want me to plug him?" Grat asked. "You've got every reason. Two of your herders are dead because of these three."

"Every reason," Jessie agreed. "But I think I'd rather take him and the dead bodies to Raines. I'd like Quint to hear our story." He grinned at a thought. "You know how suspicious Quint is. It'd stop his finger from pointing at either of us."

Grat laughed. "I can't wait to see Raines's face when we walk in together."

"It'll set him back," Jessie said, chuckling.

Grat stepped to the cave's mouth and bellowed for some of his riders. When they came up, he sent them for the three horses in the wood. "You know where we found the first one tied. There'll be three tied there now. We've got use of every one of them."

He came back, and Jessie was trying to prod Curt into further explanation.

"It won't do me any good, will it?" Curt said and smiled bleakly.

"You're a damn fool," Jessie exploded, pushed beyond his endurance. "Listening to you, I'm convinced you weren't the one who thought up all of this trouble. It could go easier with you."

Curt shook his head, his teeth set. Grat came up to overhear the last of the conversation, and he said in disgust, "It's enough to make you want to shoot him between the eyes and get this over with."

Curt thought he meant it, for he paled.

"No," Jessie said. "I haven't got the mastermind. I'm hoping Raines can put more pressure on him to make him talk."

"Whatever you want to do is all right with me," Grat said. "I've sent for their horses. We'll need them to get the two bodies and him into town."

It took a few minutes for the three horses to arrive. Jessie stood there, glaring at Curt. What kind of a man could go out and shoot down two herders, then wantonly destroy hundreds of sheep? The more he looked at the man, the greater his temper rose. He wouldn't want to be around this man much, for he couldn't guarantee his control.

"Hey, Grat," a voice called from outside. "The horses are here."

"We need some help to get the dead ones out of here," Grat called back.

Four men came in, picked up Royal and Young, and carried them outside.

Jessie intently watched Curt. Seeing his companions being carried out should do something to break him. Nothing showed on Curt's face. Curt was in as rough a spot as a man could be in, but he endured it. He was going to be a tough nut to crack.

"We're ready, Grat," a voice called.

Grat motioned with his rifle. "I guess we're ready to go in. Outside, mister. You be damned careful. I'm just looking for an excuse to empty this rifle into you."

Jessie picked up two rifles and followed Curt and Grat. Curt's hands were held high. He looked briefly at the two bodies slung across two of the horses. They were face down, and their hands and feet were tied together with pieces of rawhide taken from the saddlebags.

"Get up," Grat said coldly. "Put your hands on the horn."

He took another strip of rawhide and tied Curt's hands and lashed them to the horn.

"You trying to cut off my hands?" Curt complained.

"Tough," Grat said unfeelingly. "You don't know how lucky you are to still be breathing." He glanced at Jessie as he passed him. "Just looking at him makes me want to puke."

Jessie nodded his understanding. He felt the same way.

"Fall in around him," Grat ordered. "Don't take your eyes off him. If he even looks like he's thinking of trying to make a break, riddle him."

Heads around Curt's horse nodded soberly. Their tempers were a little on the thin side. They were tired and drained by the events of the last twenty-four hours.

Grat was satisfied, and he waved his arm forward. "Let's move out."

CHAPTER 24

Raines was at his window when the small cavalcade of riders turned onto the street running by his office. His eyes bugged out at the sight of the two riders in the van. Grat Hagen and Jessie Kilmer were in the lead, and they didn't look as though they were ready to jump at each other's throat. His amazement grew as he saw the rider in the midst of the procession. That rider's hands were lashed to the horn of his saddle. Raines's amazement grew at the sight of the two dangling bodies. Jesus Christ! There must have been a small war going on.

He dashed outside and was waiting when Grat and Jessie drew up. "What the hell's been going on?" he spluttered. "Who are those three men?"

"Interesting story goes with them," Grat said. "Those three are the ones who have been causing Jessie so much trouble. But you wouldn't listen to him. You were too damned smart for that. Me and Jessie did a little looking around and picked them up. Looks like you're too old to do your job right, Quint."

Raines spluttered and choked before he exploded, "Damn you, Grat Hagen. Don't get smart with me. I never did refuse to listen to Jessie. Did I, Jessie?" Jessie's nod didn't pacify him. "I just said he was on the wrong track. How come you two are riding together? You better get inside. You've got a lot of explaining to do."

Grat chuckled in obvious delight. "Thought you'd feel that way." He faced his riders. "Untie them, boys. Quint, what do you want done with the dead ones?"

"Bring them inside until I get this straightened out." His face grew grimmer as he watched men cut the lashings on the two bodies, then release the thongs binding the rider to his horse.

He waited until all of them were inside. He sat down in his chair, his eyes stern. "Now, suppose you tell me what this is all about. You can start by explaining why you two are riding together. You look like old-time buddies."

"Not old-time," Grat said thoughtfully. "But as good as we can ever be. Jessie saved my life last night. Not only mine but Gary's and Wirt's."

Raines's eyes grew round. "Something's been going on that I don't know anything about," he said querulously. "Now, how did all this lifesaving business come about?"

"You wouldn't know about it," Jessie said gravely. "I had a flock of sheep dynamited last night. My herder wasn't killed. He stayed inside his wagon until he felt fairly sure enough to come out. All he found was mangled sheep. He hitched up and drove to the house to let me know what had happened. I went back with him and found all those dead sheep. I knew who was behind it. The Hagens had used dynamite last year to open up a creek to get water to a piece of low ground. It wasn't any use coming to you. You'd only back the Hagens. You'd done it before."

Raines colored at the accusation in Jessie's words. "I only said there wasn't any proof. There wasn't, was there?" he finished.

Jessie grinned faintly. "There wasn't any this time, either. But I raised all the available men I had and took out for the Hagens'. I'm not saying what would have happened if I found them." He grimaced and shook his head. "When we got there, their house was afire. Burning real good. I checked to see if anybody was trapped inside." He paused, his face reflective. "Lord, how wrong a man can be and still be positive he's right."

"Go on," Raines said impatiently.

"I found Grat just coming out of his room. His face was dazed. I got him outside, then looked for more. Gary and Wirt were still inside, both of them unconscious. It was a good thing we got there when we did. We barely got them outside when the house collapsed." He winced at the memory.

"How did this fire start?" Raines asked.

"That was due to my chuckle-headed brother," Grat said in disgust. "We'd been drinking. Gary replenished the fire and left the stove door open. An ember missed the metal carpet beneath the stove, and it smoldered on the plank floor until it got a start."

Raines looked amazed. "Weren't any of you around to keep an eye on the fire?"

It was Grat's turn to look sheepish. "I told you we were drinking. We'd just made a good sale. All of us got pretty drunk celebrating. Even the hands were drunk in their bunkhouse."

"God Almighty," Raines said in a muted voice.

"So you see, Jessie saved my life. I'll never be able to pay him back."

"You already have," Jessie said stoutly. "It was your idea that let us find the cave those three used. I'd never found it without your help."

"You got any proof of what you're saying?" Raines looked stern.

"All in the world. There was only one man in the cave when we discovered it. A sprained ankle laid him up." Jessie shook his head. "He wasn't much and damned scared. We started firing questions at him, and he broke. He claimed the other two did all the damage to my sheep. He said the bum ankle kept him from going along. We found out the other two were coming back, and we waited. They walked right into our arms. The big one got into a quarrel with the small one, and the small one admitted he'd told us what they had been doing. The big one cut him down right there. He tried to whirl to gun his way out, but Grat was watching him too close. He killed the big one." Jessie shrugged. "Result? Two dead men."

"How come you brought this one in?" Raines asked.

"He decided he didn't want to die right then. He ain't very cooperative. Didn't tell us very much."

Raines got up from his chair and walked over to Curt. "What's your name, mister?" His expression was menacing.

"Curt."

"Curt ain't enough," Raines snapped. "Come on with the rest of it."

Curt shrugged and remained stubbornly silent.

"One of the hard ones," Raines said in outrage. "Why did you do it? Did somebody pay you to start the war again between the cattlemen and sheepmen?"

Curt grinned mockingly at him.

Raines was getting madder. One could tell by the shade of color in his cheeks. "You're only making it worse for yourself. We've already got you dead to rights."

Again that mocking grin that so enraged Raines.

"Did you see what he has in his pockets?" Raines asked.

Jessie shook his head. "He had a pistol and a rifle. We took them. We didn't search his pockets."

"Might as well look," Raines said. "Might be some kind of identification. If we can find out who he is, it might give us an idea who's been back of him."

Curt pulled away from Raines, his face going taut. "You can't search me," he said in a tight voice. "I've got some rights."

"You ain't got no rights of any kind," Raines said brutally. He cocked an eye at Jessie and Grat. "Keep him covered. Shoot him if he tries to resist."

The resistance drained out of Curt, and his color turned ashen.

"Hold up your arms," Raines ordered. "Everybody here is tired of fooling with you. You could pick your dying time right now."

Curt slowly raised his arms and held them out.

Raines went through the right-hand pocket of the jacket, then the opposite. His face was a study as he withdrew the hand. It was filled with money. "I'll be goddamned," he said slowly. "Would you look at this?" He quickly counted the money. "Three thousand dollars. Somebody was paying him for what he did." A thought occurred to him, and his eyes gleamed. "Maybe those dead ones had money in their pockets too. Jessie, go take a look."

Jessie's face was awed when he looked up and held up a hand. It looked as though his big fist was stuffed with money. "Quint, you hit that right on the head. Each one of them had two thousand dollars in their pockets."

"A big man was behind them," Raines said reflectively. "You want to tell us about it now? It could go a little easier on you."

Curt's lips were a tight, pressed line.

"He still doesn't want to talk," Raines said. "I like these tough ones who think they can stand up against the law. Jessie, I know you thought I wasn't doing anything. But I have been combing the town with a fine-toothed comb, trying to find out if any strangers had recently been in town. I found out where they stayed a short while. Bring him along. I think maybe some of the merchants they bought stuff from will identify him as one of the buyers."

He reached into his desk and pulled out a pair of handcuffs and snapped them on Curt's wrists. "Just to take any fool ideas of making a break out of his head."

They ushered Curt to the dowdy little store. A fat man waddled up to greet them, and the joviality slipped off his face as he saw Curt.

"So you know him, Sam," Raines said. "You better tell me what you know about him. I don't like the way you been running your business. This could be enough for me to close you down for good."

The fat man went all to pieces. Sweat broke out all over him. "I didn't do anything wrong, Sheriff," he pleaded. "Just trying to run my business the best I can. I was only trying to make an honest living."

"Not enough," Raines snapped. "Do you know this man?"

Sam's eyes flicked uneasily over Curt. He hesitated a long moment.

"He's involved in two murders," Raines said softly. "Plus the destruction of property. He's facing the stiffest kind of charges. Do you want to be included?"

That finished breaking the fat man. "He's been in here before with two others. One a big man, the other one on the insignificant side. I sold each of them a rifle and a handgun. I didn't know they were up to anything like that."

Raines eyed him ominously. "But if you had known, it wouldn't have stopped you from making a few dollars, would it, Sam?"

Sam shook all over, and the sweat ran more profusely. "You can't blame me for just running my business," he said in weak defiance.

"We'll see about that later," Raines said. "Don't you try to run. You hear me?"

"I hear you," the fat man said through trembling lips.

"We're getting somewhere," Raines said with satisfaction as they left the store.

"We didn't learn a damned thing," Jessie said forlornly.

"You didn't," Raines jeered. "I think the tracks are becoming plainer. I think we're onto something. We stop next at the Drovers' Hotel."

"I wouldn't keep a dog in there," Grat said contemptuously.

"If a man was broke, the Drovers' rates are appealing," Raines said reasonably.

They entered the sorry hotel, and Raines had to shake the desk clerk out of a doze. "Hey, Clem, wake up. I want some information."

The old man stared blearily at the people clustered before his desk. "Go ahead. Ask it," he said in a wheezing voice.

"Ever see this one before?" Raines pushed Curt forward.

Clem peered at him, then shook his head. "Never saw him before."

Raines's disappointment was visible. "Are you positive? Didn't he stay here sometime back? A week or ten days?"

Clem rubbed his eyes, then stood and leaned over the counter for a closer look. He peered at Curt for a long moment, then said, his voice steadying, "You're right, Sheriff. He stopped here. Not for very long, though. I got his name, or the name he gave me on my books."

"Can you find it, Clem?"

Clem spluttered indignantly. "You think I'm too old to remember anything." He turned a few pages of an ancient ledger, muttering to himself. "Yes! Here it is. I knew I remembered." He turned the ledger so that Raines could read it. A black-edged fingernail pointed out the entry.

"This is interesting," Raines exclaimed. "A Curt Keeley registered for room one ten. The date?" He read out the numeral. "Wasn't that before your trouble started, Jessie?"

"It was," Jessie said, going tense. Maybe Raines was better than Jessie gave him credit for.

"Does that name mean anything to you, Jessie?"

"The last name is the same as our bank's president, Jacob Keeley."

"Could he be behind all this?" Raines asked.

Jessie gave him a troubled frown. "I don't know, Quint. I know I'm due to make a payment on a loan to the bank."

"When's that?"

"The first of May," Jessie answered.

"What happens if you miss it?"

"The bank could foreclose," Jessie replied slowly. "He sure as hell can now. With all our losses, there's no way we can make it."

Curt listened to the conversation with an impassive face, but the corners of his mouth kept twitching.

"Care to explain the likeness of the last names?" Raines asked.

Curt tried to laugh, and it came out a hollow sound. "Because we have the same name doesn't mean a damned thing."

"Maybe not, maybe yes," Raines mused. "But it's a coincidence that can't be overlooked. What room did you say he had, Clem?"

"Room one ten. He's still got it. He wanted me to hold it for him."

"Has it got a key?" At the clerk's nod, Raines extended a hand. "Give it to me. I'd like to look that room over."

Jessie didn't see what good that would do, but he didn't voice his objection. Raines might be an old dog, but he could reason out a trail.

Raines unlocked door 110, shoved Curt inside, then followed him in. Grat and Jessie were right behind him. "Look around," Raines said. "Do you see anything you could hide something in?"

Grat and Jessie made a survey of the room, then shook their heads. "No place to hide anything," Grat commented.

"I got a fool idea in my head," Raines said. "I won't tell you now what it is. I don't want you laughing at me."

"Come on, tell us," Jessie insisted.

Raines shook his head. "Not now." He walked around the room, peering at everything. He crossed the room again and again, and each time he did a floorboard creaked dolorously. "That's the fourth time that board's squeaked," Raines commented. His eyes brightened as he looked at Curt.

"Something down there making you nervous, Curt?"

Curt shook his head, and he wouldn't take his eyes off the floor.

"Something's bothering him," Raines decided. "That idea is getting stronger in my head. Grat, you and Jessie are heavier than me. Walk back and forth across this loose board."

He nodded with satisfaction as Grat's and Jessie's tread produced the same squeak. "That board's loose. Maybe it's a natural thing, and maybe it isn't."

Raines kneeled beside the board, pulled a knife out of his pocket and opened a blade. He inserted the point in the crack between the two boards and pried on it. He cursed vehemently as the blade broke. He looked up and said, "One of you loan me your knife?"

"And have you break it the same way?" Grat jeered.

Jessie shook his head. "I didn't bring one."

Raines inspected the stub of a blade. "Maybe this will do as good. It's stouter this way."

He rammed the stub of the blade as far as he could get it into the crack, then pried more cautiously. The nails squealed in protest as they were forced out of their position. The board came all at once, the nails flew out, and the end of the board was a good two inches above the floor.

Raines leaned on it, bending it back until it broke with a sharp snap. Raines tossed the broken piece of board from him.

Jessie watched him with interest. Whatever Raines had in mind bothered him like fleas on a dog. Jessie couldn't even guess what it was.

Raines looked into the exposed space and dipped his hand into it. "Would you look at this?" Raines crowed. He lifted his hand, and it was stuffed with money. He laid the bills beside him, then his hand went back for another fistful. "I guess that's all," he said. He counted the money and whistled. "A little over seven thousand dollars. Now, that asks an interesting question. This Curt is a walking bank. Where would he get that kind of money?" Those old eyes flamed as he looked at Curt.

Curt was sick. It showed in his face. Still, he slowly shook his head.

"It won't do you any good to keep silent now," Raines purred. "You're already in over your head. Somebody bought you off. Do you want to tell me all about it, or do you want to go it alone? Keeping still won't help you any. It might, and I'm saying might, ease up on you if you tell me who's behind you."

He sighed as he looked at Curt. "Still stubborn, are you? Let me do a little guessing. Where would the amount of money you had on you and in this room come from? You've got the same name as our banker. I'd say the bank would be a likely place to pick up some tracks."

Curt moaned softly, but his lips were still a tight line.

Raines got to his feet. He looked like a wolf with his fangs bared. "All right, we'll play it your way. We're going to the bank and see if Jacob Keeley knows anything about all this."

He stuffed the money into his pocket and shoved Curt ahead of him. "With all this money I'm carrying, I'm going to have to have a lawman to protect me."

"I could recommend one," Jessie said. "I'd recommend Quint Raines."

"I'll second that," Grat said seriously.

Raines put a sorrowful look on his face. "Now that you two have joined up against me, life won't be worth living." He pushed Curt through the door. "Come on, mystery man. We got some more tracking to do."

He left the clerk the key. "Clem, room one ten is in a hell of a shape. Board in the floor broken right off."

Raines was still chuckling as they left the hotel.

Several people stopped and gawked at them as they made their way to the bank. A couple showed inclination of coming over and talking, but Raines waved them off.

They walked into the bank without Benson seeing them. His head was lowered as he worked at some figures.

"Charley, all you do is work," Raines said solemnly as he reached the cage. "If a man keeps at it long enough, it'll kill him." He winked at Jessie and Grat. Raines's high good humor was still holding.

He held up a hand, stopping Benson's outburst. "Just listen. I'll ask all the questions. Did you ever see this man before?" He grabbed one of Curt's manacled arms and tugged him forward.

Benson's face showed distress. Something was happening here, and he didn't know what it was. "Just once," he said in a strained voice.

"Ah," Raines said in satisfaction. "When?"

Benson licked lips that had suddenly gone dry.

"Don't try to protect Mr. Keeley," Raines said sternly. "It could pull you down into a hole you never would get out."

"He came in to see Mr. Keeley," Benson said through trembling lips.

"Did you know his name is Keeley, the same as Jacob's?"

Benson shook his head. "I didn't know that." His protestation was so genuine that Raines didn't argue with him. "Did Jacob draw any money out of the bank recently, sums that you can't explain?"

Benson looked as though he would shrivel up. "He did," he said faintly. "About ten days ago, he drew out ten thousand dollars and left a loan form made out to a Summerskill. I never heard that name before."

"Any more unexplained sums?" Raines purred. The gleam in his eyes burned brighter. The tracks were plainer than ever. A blind man could have read them.

"He took five thousand dollars out of the bank the same day this one was in," Benson said feebly.

"He didn't explain it," Raines went on relentlessly.

"He told me not to worry about it, that he was good for it," Benson whimpered. "I couldn't question him, could I?"

"You couldn't," Raines said solemnly. "We'll do that for you. Is Jacob in his office?"

Benson looked as though his legs would no longer support him. "Is Mr. Keeley in trouble?"

"Deep trouble," Raines assured him. "Don't look so worried. You're not in it. That door over there Jacob's office?"

At Benson's weak nod, Raines turned Curt toward the door. Curt opened his mouth, but before he could speak, Raines said, "I wouldn't. I'll do all the talking." He pushed Curt toward the door Benson pointed out and turned the knob.

Jacob looked up from his desk at their entrance. The frown forming on his face faded as he caught sight of Curt. "What's he doing here?" His face had paled, and he could hardly form the words.

"I think you know, Jacob," Raines said softly. "I know all about the money you took out of the bank. And I know what you did with it."

Jacob was on his feet, and he would have fallen if he hadn't grabbed at his desk for support. "You goddamned traitor," he screamed at Curt. "You told them all about it. I thought I could depend on my brother."

Curt sadly shook his head. "You just betrayed yourself, Jacob. I didn't say anything about our arrangement. But *you* did."

Jacob's eyes were stricken as he looked at Raines.

"That's right, Jacob," Raines said with immense satisfaction. "I think you'd better come along with me."

Jacob's face was whiter than new-fallen snow. "What are you going to do with me?" he whimpered.

"You should be able to guess that," Raines said in a withering voice. "You've got a lot of charges to meet. First, there's embezzlement, then a conspiracy to murder, plus destroying another man's property. Then, there's the one of trying to stir up the old hatred. Don't worry about where you're going. You're going to be there a long time. Unless the judge doesn't think you're worth throwing into prison. Then you'll hang." He turned his head and looked at Jessie and Grat. "I didn't bring another pair of handcuffs with me. Will you two see that he's delivered to the jail?"

"With pleasure," Grat and Jessie said in unison. They walked on each side of him, escorting him to the door. Every now and then Jessie was tempted to throw out a hand to keep Jacob from falling to the floor. Jacob's knees insisted upon buckling.

The last thing he saw before they left the bank was Benson staring wide-eyed at them. Jessie shook his head sorrowfully at him. Not for what was happening to Jacob, but for the old man. This abrupt change in his life was going to be rough on him.

CHAPTER 25

Raines came back after locking up the two Keeleys, and he was grinning from ear to ear. "When I left, they were screaming at each other. They sounded like two tomcats getting ready for a battle. Lucky the bars separated them."

"What will happen to Jacob, Quint?" Jessie asked.

"If he doesn't hang, he'll spend the rest of his life in prison. Don't feel any sorrow for him. He's earned it. I'd almost say with certainty that Curt will hang." He sat down. "Isn't it odd what happens to men? Jacob was the last one I would have picked to be involved in this. I guess greed is one common weakness in all of us. Forget about that loan, Jessie. It'll be wiped out. I'm positive of that. No sane judge would ever rule any other way. I've got a hunch the money Jacob handed over to Curt will be given to you. You've earned that for squashing a possible breakout of the old war. It'd only make up your losses. But don't quote me. I'm no judge." He grinned in amusement. "I'm just a jug-headed sheriff."

Jessie squirmed uncomfortably. "You'll never let me forget that, will you?"

"Never," Raines promised. "I do owe you a debt of gratitude. I won't have to worry about you two getting into a fight again."

"Never," Grat said with conviction. "After what Jessie did for me, he could spit in my eye, and I'd offer him the other one."

Jessie's uncomfortableness increased. "Will you cut it out, Grat?"

Raines leaned back, thoroughly relaxed. "Both of you owe appreciation to the other. I don't think either of you will ever forget it."

"Do you enjoy listening to this, Jessie?" Grat asked.

"Hell, no." Jessie was thinking of Asa. Asa didn't know the aftermath of all this. God, how relieved Asa would be. He had earned the right to a little peace.

"Then let's get out of here, Jessie. How about a drink? I'd enjoy buying you one."

"And I'd enjoy having that drink," Jessie replied. "Should we ask Quint? He earned a little credit in all this."

Grat pretended deep study, then said reluctantly, "All right, if you want to ask him. I guess I could stand him being around us a little more."

"Not me," Raines refused. "I've got a long report to make out about this. A piece of advice to you two. Hold it down. Not more than three drinks. As hair-triggered as your tempers are, the next thing you know, you'd be slinging fists."

Jessie looked pained. "Did you hear that, Grat? He didn't pay any attention to anything we told him."

"Hardheaded old cuss, ain't he?" Grat said as he shook his head.

They walked to the door together, stopped there and looked back. "Quint, once again our thanks."

"Will you get out of here?" Raines growled. "Can't you see that I'm busy?"

Jessie and Grat strolled down the street together, both of them grinning broadly. "Pretty good ole boy," Jessie said.

"I never thought I'd agree with you," Grat said. "But I can't argue with you."

They passed Brown's saloon without pausing, and Jessie said, "Hey! Isn't that your favorite drinking hole?"

"Used to be," Grat replied. He had a smug look that should have worried Jessie. "There's another saloon a couple of blocks farther on. I think you'll like it."

They turned a corner, and Jessie's eyes narrowed. This street was leading out of the business district. There were no saloons here. "Hey," Jessie cried. "This is all residential district. What are you trying to pull, Grat?"

"Just another half block," Grat said soothingly. "Trust me. You don't think I'd do anything that would harm you, do you?"

"I don't know what to think anymore." Jessie's eyes started to burn. He should. He had been here often enough.

He grabbed Grat's arm. "I don't know what you're up to," he said, "but I don't like the looks of it."

"Never knew a meaner, more suspicious mind," Grat said defensively. "Will it kill you to step in for a minute or two? That's all I'm asking."

Jessie swallowed hard. He couldn't refuse Grat, not when he put it that way. His heart started aching. Beth Cagel lived in this house. Was Grat trying to rub his nose in his disillusion? No, he tried to think stoutly. Grat wouldn't do something like that.

Beth answered Grat's knock, and her eyes flashed as she looked at Grat, then heated as they flicked to Jessie. "What are the two of you doing here?" she asked coldly. "I have no reason to want to see either of you."

"You've got every reason to see Jessie," Grat said easily. "Is he still steamed up about that dance? Hell, you had no room for me at all. You cut me down real good. Make him understand that." He grinned lazily at Jessie. "You listen to her, boy. It's all for your own good." He tipped his hat to Beth and turned and strolled down the walk. His whistling drifted back to them.

Beth still stared defiantly at Jessie. "Well," she demanded.

"You called me stupid once. Looks like you were right. I jump at appearances without even trying to find what's behind them."

Her frosty expression was beginning to melt. "Maybe I shouldn't have said 'stupid.' But you'll have to admit you're a little slow grasping things."

Jessie stubbornly shook his head. "No, I think stupid fits just right."

She almost laughed and managed to bite it back in time. "Seeing you and Grat together surprised me no end. Is there peace between you two now?"

"Forever, Beth," he said solemnly. "I was all wrong in accusing Grat of the trouble I've had recently."

Beth cocked her head to one side. "He must have been persuasive in making you think differently. What happened?"

Jessie colored. "I blew my top at the loss of more sheep. Raines had told me that the Hagens had nothing to do with it. I didn't believe him. I tore out to the Hagens'. If I had found them outside their house, I don't know what would have happened. But the house was on fire. I looked to be sure everybody was out. Grat was just coming out of a room, dazed and sick. I got him out, then found his younger brother and father. I had enough help to get all of them out."

She looked curiously at him. "Then you two will never be enemies again?"

"Never," he said emphatically. "Grat helped me find out who was behind the destruction of my sheep. You'd never believe this, Beth, but it was Jacob Keeley."

"No," she gasped, her eyes rounded.

He nodded soberly. "Yes. He wanted to foreclose on my land, and he could have if his plan worked. I had a loan coming up next month. There was no way I could have met it."

"That was what was on your mind the day we met outside the lumber yard."

"A lot of it was," he confessed. "Beth, I'm sorry for all the misery I caused you. Will you give me a new chance?"

Her smile started at her lip corners, then spread until her face glowed with it. Her eyes were dancing. "Oh, Jessie, if you knew how miserable I've been. You're the one who should be giving me another chance."

He opened his arms, and she came into them. He bent his head to kiss her, and a thought popped into his head. Asa knew what he was talking about when he said that someday Jessie would want his interest on the land to be extended to an offspring. Asa was a wise old bird. Again, Jessie had learned that Asa knew what he was talking about.